Paradise Found

Dahlia Rose

Amira Press, LLC

Paradise Found
Dahlia Rose

ISBN: 978-1-934475-44-7

Publisher:
Amira Press, LLC
Baltimore, MD
www.amirapress.com

Paradise Found
Dahlia Rose

Prologue

He liked it best when they were scared, too scared to speak. He looked across the semi-lighted room to the waif-like figure he had tied to the bed. Arms outstretched tied to each post of the bed. He had dressed her just the way he remembered from long ago, from the first time. This one had the eyes that he liked, big, wide, and scared, like an animal trapped with no escape. He'd watched her for a whole week learning her routes to and from classes she took at Central Piedmont College. He knew it all—where she lived, whom she chose to be friends with, even the idiot boy who she had decided to let be her boyfriend. She was so easy to catch. He liked that word, catch. *Come into my web said the spider to the fly,* he thought with a smile. Now look at her lying there eyes looking at him with a mixture of despair and dread. She felt her skin crawl as he touched her face in a caress, the blood drained from her face as she looked at him. She was thinking, "Oh my God, I'm going to be raped." But he soon put that thought to rest. It was never about sex for him. With his looks and his charm, he had no problems getting a woman when he wanted one, knew he could when he needed to. Plus, she had not angered him to have that kind of punishment inflicted on her, but he would make her his in his own way, a way that was most special. They would share a very special bond when this was through, and she would be blessed forever for giving him what he needed.

He walked over to her and sat on the edge of the bed. The saggy mattress dipped low because of his weight, and she instantly began to struggle, knowing that something bad was going to happen to her. His touch was soft against her face, and he caressed her cheek. "Don't worry, dove," he said softly to her all the while his hand still against her cheek. "This is a special gift you are giving to me, and I promise you there will be no pain, but it must be done, and I'll carry you with me forever." He watched her eyes, and she finally understood that her life would end that night to sustain his. First came the denial, followed by her eyes begging for a reprieve, then came slow acceptance of her fate. He liked that part the best, when they gave in to what they were meant to do just for him. He soothed and talked to her as he inserted a needle in her arm and watched her eyes go from life filled to dull as the essence drained from her. He laid his head against her chest and listened. Her heartbeat slowed, slowed until the last thud echoed through him like a drum in an empty room. He sighed in pleasure and then began his work to make her process and his transformation complete.

Chapter One

"Come on, Kelly, why do you go running at that park when you can run around here?" Abby asked. Abigail Hobart was her upstairs neighbor and closest friend. For years, they lived on two continents, then two different states, but the distance never made the friendship any less than what it always was, from five-year-old children to now, best friends forever. Then finally, after visits and talks over the telephone, they now lived stairs away from each other.

"Because I like that park," Kelly answered simply. She sat on her overstuffed chair, pulled on her running shoes, and checked her essentials for a good run. Music-check, water-check, and keys-check. She was ready to go.

"It's a gated complex. I would feel much safer…" Abby began.

Kelly grabbed her friend's pigtails and gave her a smacking kiss on the lips. "I'll be fine, just like I was fine on Monday and the Friday before, stop worrying."

Abby gave up with a sigh. She knew it was no use to argue with her. "Fine but you run your butt up these stairs and let me know when you get back."

"That will be the first thing I do since I have a date tonight and I need my black dress back," Kelly called as she ran out the door. "Lock up on your way out will you?" She heard the faint reply from Abby who was now intently going through her shoes in her closet and smiled to herself as she crossed the street and speed walked to the park.

This was always her favorite time of day to run, just before the sunset and the night took over. It was autumn which in Kelly's book was another added bonus. Gone were those long humid days that Charlotte was known for. The evenings were crisp and cool, the leaves fell in an array of colors and as she ran Kelly wanted to turn in circles and just marvel at the beauty of it. Her long hair, which was black with bronze streaks, was pulled back into a high ponytail, and even with her iPod on and the music on, she felt a laugh bubble up from inside her. Her decision to move from New York to North Carolina was a good one. She had gotten tired of the busy streets and the never-ending noise and traffic of Manhattan. Having grown up in wide-open spaces with trees and grass, and after visiting Abby, she fell in love instantly and made the decision to relocate. Now, running in Freedom Park with the autumn color all around her, she reaffirmed this was the best decision she ever made.

She rounded the curve in the park for the second time where the road leads around by the wire fence of the military base that was right next to the park. She skidded to a stop, and with Rob Zombie blasting in her ears, she watched the scene unfold in front of her like the gruesome part of a horror movie, the part that makes you cover your eyes and try to peek through your fingers because you can't look away. A man was holding a woman against the fence. She was limp as if unconscious. What was he doing to that poor girl on the fence?

"Hey, stop that! Leave her alone!" Kelly yelled, absolutely ready to use what little she knew from kickboxing to defend the defenseless girl, her mind was going a mile a minute. *Okay, he's way bigger than you,* Kelly thought. *But you can, fuck what can you do? He would squish you.* But if the girl is in trouble, she had to try to do something. Her voice startled the man from his task, and he whirled around to face her, then she saw the true horror of what was happening. The girl was deathly pale, her face perfectly made up, but her eyes blank and staring. Her dress was open at the front, revealing a large gash on her chest, and he had her tied onto the fence as if she were kneeling in prayer with her cold, dead eyes staring up at him in adoration. Kelly caught his movement in the dead girl's eyes. He was coming toward her, his body tense, ready to strike and take her down. Kelly tried to jump back, but it was too late. He caught her around the waist, and she landed on the grass. She was not ready for this day, not ready to face an unknown assailant, not ready to die. All the self-defense training she had learned fled from her mind, and Kelly did the only thing that came to her. She screamed like she never had before in her life, and she kicked and scratched and fought like a woman possessed. Finally, she was able to gouge him in the eye, causing him enough pain to grab for his face, and give Kelly the break she needed.

She scrambled up off the ground and screamed like the devil was after her. She kept screaming because she knew that in that instant, her life depended on it. She screamed as she ran. She didn't even look behind her to see if he was following. She kept screaming until she got to the road and saw the police car coming, even then it took a hard shake from the police officer to get her to stop the noise and to tell him what she saw and what had happened to her. The cop looked at her, could see something was wrong from her grass-stained clothes and the pieces of grass in her hair.

They walked back, and in her mind, what she had seen replayed. They came upon the girl in her position of prayer, and before the officer called it in, she heard him gasp, "My God." She sat there in shock and disbelief as the serene park she ran in became overrun with police and investigators and helicopters in the sky. The park, now brightly lit, had an area taped off with that yellow police tape she had ever only seen on television shows. Trying to catch a glimpse of what was going on, hoping to snap up any juicy bits of information that they could pass on to the public via live feed, the press stood outside the plastic barrier, only being told that an unidentified woman had been found dead. "Who would do this?" and "My God, look at her chest," were some of the passing comments from some of the police that passed back and forth.

Who would do this! she thought angrily. *Some sick freak, that's who!* She felt numb as they wrapped a blanket around her and asked if she needed to go to the hospital. Kelly refused so they placed her in a car and took her to police headquarters uptown to take her statement. At headquarters, she passed face after face, and each stopped to look at her. The news about the woman who had been found had already spread. Kelly could not tell you what anyone looked like. She was just seeing what was in her mind over and over again, replaying like a tape stuck on rewind in her head. They put her in a gray room and left her there sitting alone. Kelly put her head on the metal desk and closed her eyes, but quickly opened them again as the girl's face popped into her head. Just then, the door to the room opened, and a tall man walked in. Compared to Kelly, at five-three, he was at least six-two, she thought, with a muscular build and a face like a bulldog. In his hand, he carried two cups.

* * * *

Daniel Greywood had been a detective for the CHPD for about ten years. He knew this community, and he had seen murders, some gruesome, some that broke his heart, but in ten years, he had never seen anything like what he saw tonight. He looked at the tiny thing sitting at the desk. When he opened the door, she'd jumped like a scared cat, almost tipping the chair over as she sprang to her feet.

"Please, sit down. I'm sorry if I startled you. Hi, I'm Detective Greywood," he said. "And you are Kelly?"

"Detective Greywood for the gray room."

He looked at her after that comment as he sat down.

"Sorry, I make bad jokes when I'm nervous or frightened, both of which I am right now. I'm Kelly, um, Kelly Justine."

"No problem, Ms. Justine, after what you saw tonight and being attacked you have every right to be both," Detective Greywood responded. "Coffee?" he asked as he slid a cup across the table to her.

"Um, no. I'm trying not to drink it anymore. Bit of a coffee addict."

But even as she said it, she reached out and took the cup from his hand. Detective Greywood smiled as she lifted the cup to her nose and inhaled. He could tell the smell alone was enough to make her break her promise to herself. She had had a hell of an evening. He thought she deserved a cup anyway. It was squad-room coffee. It would taste awful but at least it was caffeine.

"You have an accent, Ms. Justine. Where are you from?" He had asked casually, knowing it was better to get her relaxed before he asked what she saw at the park. She'd remember more, and he'd get some background in the process.

"Call me Kelly. I'm from Barbados. Then I moved to London when I was a child, hence the accent."

"Wow, well, what are you doing in little Charlotte?"

"I lived in New York, and then I moved here because the big city was becoming a bit much." As she talked he saw her begin to relax and then he knew he could ask her some vital questions.

"Kelly, what did you see tonight?"

"I was running, I do that three time a week in the park to keep fit, you know what I mean, I also kick box," she added hastily.

Detective Greywood let her ramble. He knew it would be best because she would be more detailed.

"I saw this guy standing by the fence, I thought he was relieving himself but then I saw the girl's feet. I thought he was raping her and I was totally prepared to kick his ass if he was."

"Very brave of you," he said amused but trying not to show it. She was small, and she thought she could kick someone's ass.

"So I shouted and told him to stop. He turned around, and then I saw her face." Kelly shuddered.

"She looked so pale, and her eyes were staring at nothing. I knew, I just knew, she was not alive anymore and then I saw her . . . her chest."

"Take your time, Kelly," he said in a comforting tone. "What happened after you shouted and he turned?"

"He came towards me like . . . like he was going to grab me and . . . and before I could run, he grabbed me around the waist, and next thing I knew, I was on the ground."

He saw her take a deep breath and try to stop the tears from welling in her eyes before continuing. "I fought him. I wasn't ready to die, and I guess I caught him in the eye with my nails."

She showed the detective her hands. He noticed the purple nail polish on perfectly manicured nails and nodded slowly waiting for her to finish her story.

"I ran, and I just started screaming. I guess it startled him because he stopped chasing me, so I just turned my ass around and ran screaming until I flagged down the patrol car."

"Can you tell me what he looked like?"

"No, he was wearing one of those ski mask thingies, like you see on the tele when they are robbers."

"Tele?"

"You know tele . . . television, TV."

"Oh, okay. What else can you tell me about him?"

"He's tall—well, taller than me anyway—but not as tall as you are like about five ten maybe and thick around the shoulders like he works out or something."

Detective Greywood wrote as she spoke taking down every little thing that she said. It was best to get it all now while it was fresh in her memory.

"What else, Kelly?" he asked gently when she stopped talking and stared off into space as if she was caught in the memory of what she saw.

"His eyes, his eyes were green but not just green, like jade. They were cold, and they were hard and angry, like he was mad I disturbed him or something."

I'll bet, the detective thought grimly. "Is there anything else?"

"I think . . . I think he was a soldier."

"Why do you say that?"

"The way he was dressed, that camouflage they wear, and even his boots were polished."

Detective Greywood sat a little taller in his chair. That piece of information made this whole case turn in a new direction.

"That's enough for now, Kelly. You've given me great things to go on here."

"Can I go?" Kelly asked

"Not quite yet. There's someone who'll need to talk to you, and then we'll get someone to take you home."

"Okay, but I have a friend at home. She'll be worrying. Can someone call her?"

"Sure, sure. Just write her name and number down, and hey, we'll even get you a sandwich to go with this God-awful coffee. Okay?"

"I guess," she replied.

He heard the exhaustion in her voice, as if she were suddenly too tired to do anything but put her head back onto that cold metal table. Danny Greywood closed the door to the interview room quietly and walked to his desk.

His partner walked up to him, a newbie to the squad named Kirk Fields. Kirk was on the force for a little less time than Danny. He'd gotten his gold shield and had asked for a transfer to the Charlotte police force in hopes of a little more action than what Huntersville offered. "The girl give you anything good?"

"Yeah, lots to go on. Now I have to make a damn call."

"Why? What about?"

"Fuck!" he said as he dialed the numbers and waited for the ring on the other end. "I think we got a soldier as a fucking murder suspect."

"God damn!" Kirk exclaimed. "You sure? Hell, is she sure?"

"She sure as hell is. She was close enough to tell me the color of his eyes, and she described his uniform."

Danny heard someone pick up at the other end of the phone and ended his conversation with his partner. He had other things to talk about with the person on the other end.

* * * *

She interrupted him. He paced the dimly lit room and swore to himself.

She interrupted the process. His beautiful dove was going to show him the adoration he deserved, and she fucking interrupted him! He threw the bottle of beer against the wall and watched the bits and pieces of glass run down the wall in the foam of the beer. *But she is beautiful,* he thought as he calmed his breathing. When she fought him, he felt the small frame she had and saw how her eyes sparkled even in the growing darkness of the night. She would be his next. She would be the one to complete his transformation, he decided. He could almost see her looking at him with eyes full of adoration and love, and she would wear the white of the dove. His pure dove.

He wasn't worried that she could identify him. His face had been sufficiently concealed. He had made sure of it. But he could find her. He had the means and the contacts to find her. He already knew her name and her address, and she hadn't even left the police station yet. He laughed to himself softly, knowing he would soon know more. After all, he was a man in a position to find out whatever he needed about his new dove. He would watch and wait patiently, and then he would take her. No one will be able to stop him then, because who can stop the immortal?

Chastising himself for his display of anger, he cleaned up the mess from the broken bottle. There was no need to be angry, he thought, settling comfortably in his chair to watch and listen. Around him, nine glass jars with nine beautiful human hearts perfectly preserved. In front of him was Sherry's heart, still pink and fresh in its new home, unlike some of the others which had gone dull from the liquid they were in and from the time that had passed. But they were beautiful to him, nonetheless. He looked at them, now silent out of the human vessels he took them from, yet he could hear them still beating, slow and rhythmically. He heard the sound like a choir singing only to him, beating just to please him.

Chapter Two

He sat on his deck watching the stars come out over the lake when the call came in. When the phone rang, the head of his big black mastiff lifted and his ears perked up.

"Heard it too, did ya, boy?" he said. He knew it had to be something if it was being patched through from his office to his home. He debated with himself whether to answer the call even as his feet moved across the deck to the sliding door of his home.

"What?" The only word from his mouth into the receiver of the phone was short and clipped. He listened while the person at the other end relayed the message

"Are you sure?" He wiped his hand over his face and felt that his beard was coming back in.

"Jesus Christ! I'll be there in forty-five. Keep her there." He hung up the phone and cursed under his breath. Walking up the stairs, he muttered, "I should've never answered the damn phone." But he knew that would have been pointless because they would have reached him regardless the method. He walked into his bedroom to change.

* * * *

Forty-seven minutes later, he pulled into police headquarters in Charlotte. He looked at his watch and shook his head. He lived on Lake Norman for goodness sake. They are lucky he was there under an hour. All eyes turned on him as he entered the building. He knew exactly where to go. Danny Greywood saw him as he crossed the room and was already on his feet by the time he got to his desk.

"Danny, nice to see you again," he said. "How's life been treating you?"

"T. J., you bastard, life is life. I just make the best of it," Danny replied with a huge grin on his face. "How's life on Lake Norman?"

"It's quiet, I'm alone, and it's what I like." As they shook hands, Danny looked into the face of an old friend, Lt. T. J. Chapel United States Army. They had been friends for years even after Danny left the military and joined the police force, and Detective Greywood knew the only guy that would be able to get a handle on this if one of his soldiers had committed the murder.

"So, tell me what made you get me off my deck?" T. J. asked

"Some nasty business here, T-man. Seems a girl was found murdered in Freedom Park, tied up on the fence next to the base there."

"Yeah, I got that, but what makes you think it's a soldier?"

"The witness we have. She saw the guy, actually caught him in the act of positioning the body. He tried to chase her, but she ran screaming and flagged down a squad car, which leads us up to now."

As T. J. listened, he looked over the files and the pictures. His face went hard and cold at what had been done to the girl in the photos. No one should have to go through something like that.

"The victim got a name?"

"Yes. We already identified her, her name is Sherry Mayes, eighteen, going to school at CCPC. Her parents have been notified, and we're trying to keep details out of the morning news. Autopsy hasn't been done yet, but the sick bastard cut her heart out after draining her body of blood, but nowhere near where he was leaving her. The guy had her all dolled up, well, you see the pictures."

"Yeah, I see. Where is the witness?"

Danny pointed to the interview room. "She's been here for hours and hasn't complained, but she's stretched to the breaking point and wants to go home."

"She can go after I finish talking with her," T. J. replied walking toward the room Danny pointed to. He looked through the glass of the door before entering. Inside, he saw an uneaten sandwich and arms full of hair.

She heard the door open and looked up. T. J. knew she was probably expecting to be told she could leave. Instead, she saw a military figure. It had to be disconcerting to see a guy dressed in his uniform standing there. *Does she have a thing for men in uniform?* He was sure he could see a womanly appreciation for him in her eyes.

"Good evening, ma'am. My name is Lieutenant T. J. Chapel," he said. T. J. saw as her mind started to wander away from him and snapped it back into the present. "Ma'am?"

"Oh, sorry, my mind went off in another direction."

"I could see that," he said brusquely. "Like I said I'm Lieutenant. T. J.—"

"I heard you the first time, Lieutenant."

"Well, then, let's get to it," he said. "You are Kelly Justine, twenty-nine years old, born in Barbados moved to the U. K. when you were sixteen, went to school there, and earned a degree in English, which you don't seem to use. You currently reside in the Camden Apartments, you live alone, and your parents live in New York. Is that correct?"

"Well, gee, I guess that sums it up. What color panties am I wearing?" she asked sarcastically. The fire was back in her just as quickly as it had left.

His gaze never left her face, and he said in the same serious and business-like tone, "I wouldn't know, ma'am."

"You seem to know everything else about me so I just assumed."

"It's my business to know about you before I come in here, ma'am, and when someone accuses one of my soldiers—"

"Now wait a bloody minute! I didn't say it was one of your soldiers. I said I think it was a soldier. I didn't accuse anyone of anything. I just told them what I saw, and if it was one of *your* soldiers, he fucking attacked me. I didn't go over and say, 'Hey, throw me on the grass and try to kill me!' And for goodness sake stop calling me ma'am. I'm not sixty with a bun!"

He looked at her sitting there, her eyes shooting daggers at him and sparking with anger. She had a temper, which probably helped her get away. Her lips were drawn in a tight line, but it didn't hide the fullness of them. She was beautiful in a homespun kind of way. Her skin was beautiful, the color some kind of whipped coffee drink, and it looked just as smooth. But he wasn't here to appreciate her looks or her body. He was here to find out what she knew and get back to his lake and peace.

"Ms. Justine . . . Kelly," T. J. said in a soothing voice, trying to get back on a friendlier path with her. "I need to know why you think it was a soldier who killed that girl?"

"The way he was dressed for one. Camouflage from top to bottom and black boots."

"He could have bought those from any army surplus store," he told her.

"But his boots were shined, I mean spotless. Now I've known a few military men, and I know for a fact they keep their boots immaculate."

She's right on that point. A soldier is trained. He carries that training with him all the time, he thought. "What else, ma'am?"

"My name is Kelly, and the way he moved seemed like he was trained."

"In what way?"

"When he came at me, he didn't just come at me. He moved like slow, deliberate, bent at the knees like a predator looking for the best way to strike."

T. J. looked at her when she stopped speaking, her eyes filled with fear as she remembered the attack. Luckily, he thought, she had the presence of mind to run and scream. Some women would have been too scared to move. But she had said enough to make him wonder if a guy in the service had done this killing, and now he would have to find out.

"That's all for now, Kelly," he said as he rose to leave.

"Well, you're welcome," she said between her teeth, and he closed the door behind him.

* * * *

Detective Greywood came in right after T. J. left. He had been standing outside the doorway out of her line of sight listening to what she said to Danny.

"Thank you for your patience, Ms. Justine."

"Kelly," she repeated again. "You know I hate the way my name is beginning to sound when you guys say it. I dislike formality, even under these circumstances. Your friend was rude as hell, and when can I leave?"

"Kelly," he said, correcting himself, "I'm going to have someone drive you home in a patrol car, and if you remember anything or need anything, you can call me or Lieutenant Chapel." He gave her both cards, and she took then and slipped them into the skin of her iPod.

"The rude lieutenant could have had the manners to give me his card himself."

Danny nodded solemnly. "Yes, he could have."

"Detective, did . . . Um, did you find out her name, the girl that died I mean, what was her name?"

"Her name was Sherry," he replied, then turned and walked back into the police station.

* * * *

T. J. watched Ms. Justine being led outside, and through the glass saw her slide into the backseat of the patrol car. She stared into nothingness as the squad car pulled away slowly. Afterward, T. J. sat at Danny's desk and made a few calls. He needed some background information, and he needed it fast. Even though Kelly Justine could not give them a full description, he had a gnawing sensation in his stomach that this was a soldier, and from every indication this wasn't his first or his last killing. Danny walked up just as he was finishing his final call.

"Yeah, get that to me ASAP," he said and hung up the phone. Danny looked at him as he sat down on the other side of his desk.

"Glad to see you're making yourself comfortable," Danny said.

"You know me, I adapt to any situation." He took a sip of coffee and grimaced. "Regardless of how bad. How do you drink this swill?"

"Years of practice, plus ninety percent of my taste buds are dead."

T. J. chuckled. "See that's what you get when you become a cop. Long nights and bad coffee."

"So, what do you think, T-man? You think she saw one of yours?"

"I don't know man, but my gut is telling me it's a big possibility."

"What's your next step?"

"Well, I called for some info on any ex-military or dishonorables who have assault on their record and live in or around the neighborhood, and I'll have to wait for the autopsy report to see what else that brings up."

"What do you need from my end?"

"I hope you know, Danny, we'll have to share info until we figure out what's going on. But if this is a soldier, it will become a government case."

"Yeah, I know procedure. I haven't forgotten how this works."

"Didn't think you did. What I need is for you to find out if there are any similar murders fitting this pattern around the state or any others, we'll work from there."

"I want to be kept in the loop, T. J. This happened in my city."

"I won't keep you out of it."

"Good to know," Danny replied. "What about the witness, Kelly?"

"First-name basis already, Dan?"

"Hell, she doesn't seem big on formality. She told me to call her that.

Doesn't seem like people refuse her much."

"Really?" T. J. drawled out slowly.

Danny cleared his throat and blushed. "So what do you think?"

"She seems clearheaded enough, intelligent."

"A hell of a looker, great body." When T. J. looked at him with a raised eyebrow, Danny added hastily, "Tell me you didn't notice."

"Jesus! What were you doing, conducting an interview or giving her a physical?"

"I may be a cop, but I notice these things. I ain't dead." This conversation was getting nowhere and Danny knew T. J. did notice he just wasn't going to let on that he noticed.

"She will be fine. She didn't see his face, and his primary target was the girl. She was just in the wrong place at the wrong time. He attacked her because he thought she could ID him. She didn't get the mask off so there shouldn't be a problem." They continued to talk as T. J. got up and put on his coat. His mind was working on all the different angles, processing all the information he had.

As he walked to the door, he said, "I'm out of here for now. Call me at my office if you get anything more and as soon as the autopsy comes in."

"Will do, T-man," Danny replied.

With that, T. J. walked out into the cool night air, which smelled fresh compared to the smell of cigarette and old coffee of the station house. He let his mind wander in the direction of Ms. Kelly Justine, but shook that off almost instantly. He had no time to think about her, nor did he need the added complication in his life a woman would bring. His life was fine the way it was. It was him, alone.

* * * *

On the east side of Charlotte, the patrol car that took Kelly home was just pulling into her apartment complex. After thanking them for the ride, she slowly walked to her apartment. Unlocking the door, she looked back over her shoulder and saw the cops were still sitting in their car, waiting until she got inside. *That was so nice of them,* she thought. She waved at them to let them know she was okay. They waved back and drove off. As she closed her door behind her, Abby came rushing from the bedroom and immediately embraced her in a bone-crushing hug.

"Oh, honey! I heard all about it. It's all over the news. Are you okay?"

"I'm fine, I'm fine," she wearily reassured her friend. "What are they saying?"

"Just that a girl was killed in Freedom Park. Nothing on details."

"They didn't say someone else was attacked?"

"No, no, they didn't," Abby responded. Then she took note of Kelly's wild hair and her mussed up clothes.

"Oh God, Kelly! He attacked you!" She gasped, and at Kelly's nod, Abby hugged her once again.

"I guess the police are keeping that out of the media for now."

"What happened, Kelly? What did you see?"

"Abby, it was so horrible. She was so little and looked so innocent, and he just took that from her!"

Kelly could see on Abby's face that she knew how it affected her to see another person like that. Abby was her closest friend and knew how she was. It went beyond empathy for her. She felt things deeply, and she knew that what she had seen would hurt for a long time. She didn't even want to consider what Sherry, the girl who had been murdered, had gone through, what that girl had been forced to deal with before her death. Abby hugged her tight again while Kelly wished she could help her stop reliving it in her head.

"Do you need me to stay tonight?" Abby asked.

"No, peach, I'm good. I'm going to take the hottest shower possible and go to bed."

"You know you still call me that and I still hate it."

Kelly smiled. She had nicknamed her friend "peach" years ago for a hairstyle she had given herself that in Kelly opinion made her look like a fuzzy peach.

Kelly responded, "Yeah, I know you hate it, but you love me."

"I wonder why. Get some sleep. I'll give you a ride to work tomorrow." Abby said the statement over her shoulder as she walked through the door.

Kelly knew it was useless to argue that she could take the bus, plus she was too tired to argue anyway. She locked the door to her apartment and was stepping out of her clothes before she got to her bedroom. She stood under the hot spray of the shower until she was almost asleep. Dropping into bed naked with her hair still wet, she fell into a deep sleep almost as her head hit the pillow. In her dreams, she saw dark figures and cold, dead eyes pleading with her for help.

Chapter Three

The alarm went off too soon, and Kelly struggled out of her sleep. She opened one bleary eye and looked at the digital numbers blinking at her. It felt like she just went to sleep and the few hours of slumber were filled with the horrible images from the night before. She slid from her bed and walked, still nude, into her kitchen and looked at her coffee pot longingly. She could almost taste that hot, rich liquid on her tongue but resisted the temptation to make a pot. *Whose crazy idea was this anyway, giving up coffee?*

As she put the kettle on to make a cup of tea, she remembered it was Abby's idea saying she was coffee addicted. She made a mental note to kill her later, and then it flooded back into her memory, Sherry's death. She made another mental note not to use the word "kill" in reference to anyone ever again. She walked back to her bedroom with her cup of tea in her hand and began her morning routine to get ready for work. Kelly was closing her apartment door and her friend Abby was coming down the stairs to give her a ride to work before going to her own job. She noticed the car across the way and the person sitting on the driver's side. A chill ran through her but she shrugged it off as the chilly morning air. *Probably just another person leaving for work this morning,* she thought and put it out of her head. As the little red sports car pulled out and went out of the gated community the blue car pulled into the spot it had vacated a few moments ago.

Kelly loved her job and looked forward to going everyday, well almost everyday. Jenny and Julie Beaumont were seventy-seven year-old Southern belles and had lived together all their lives. They shared the grand old house through the years. Both married and raised their children there. When their spouses died and their children moved away, they had remained proud and beautiful, like the weeping willow tree that adorned the front yard. Except these women seemed to think that instead of being over seventy, they were seventeen. Hired by the daughters of both the ladies, Kelly served as a home aide, physical therapist, and companion. It was relatively easy until they decided to bicker about the smallest of things or go out to concerts, bars, or clubs. They had a knack for finding new things to try from salsa lessons to trying to have parties that could out do even Kelly's flair for fun. *They are no ordinary grandmas, more like Southern belles mixed with margaritas*, Kelly thought with a grin on her face. That was how she found them that morning when she walked through the front door. Nose to nose, the women stood in the foyer of the house with the aid of matching canes arguing, and neither listening to the other. Today would be a day she would have to play referee between the two.

"It should be to the left of the banister, sister!"

"Don't be daft, Julie. It looks better to the right."

"Daft! Pea-brain, Daddy always said I had the brains of the both of us."

"Daddy said that after he came home with bourbon on his breath!"

"How dare you speak of our beloved father that way?"

Kelly watched the volley back and forth with amusement. Both women, with their gray hair immaculately curled the same way, were turning red as they argued. She decided to stop the argument before they came to blows.

"Good morning, ladies," she sang out with a bright smile. "And what is the fuss on such a beautiful fall morning?"

They both looked around at the sound of her voice, and Jenny spoke up before Julie could open her mouth.

"Ah, Kelly, you shall be the deciding factor, my dear."

"And what will I be deciding today?"

Julie answered. "The hall table. I think it would look better on the left of the banister."

"Yes, yes," Jenny piped in impatiently. "Of course, I believe, and I'm sure you will too, it looks better on the right."

Kelly rolled her eyes. "And to think I stopped such a complicated debate."

"What do you think? I'm sure you agree with me," they both sang out simultaneously then stared each other down.

"With such decorative knowledge that you two share, I think that the table looks wonderful where it is now next to the banister by the hallway bathroom. You did, after all, put it there for the effect and the mirror above it."

They looked at each other again and nodded. "Quite right, of course. What were we thinking?"

Another crisis averted, Kelly thought as she shook her head. The ladies were already chattering away about doilies, needlework, and watching the MTV channel.

"Kelly, my dear, did you see the news about that horrible murder in the park?" Julie asked

Not only saw it, lived it, Kelly thought gloomily. "Yes, I did. It was terrible," she said trying to shake off the instant gloom that assaulted her.

"Horrible, just horrible!" her twin added, shaking her head.

Kelly wanted to change the subject, so she put a bright smile on her face and faced them

"Come on, ladies, let's go the kitchen and I'll make breakfast. Then it's physical therapy time, and maybe we can take a walk later before lunch. Cards in the evening. How does that sound?"

"Marvelous, but maybe instead of cards, later tonight we could go for a quick jaunt to that lovely little bar down the street?" Jenny batted her eyes as she spoke innocently.

"I don't think I am supposed to let you two out in bars anymore. Last time, you pinched that guy's butt, and he thought I was flirting with him," Kelly said.

"He shouldn't wear such tight pants if he doesn't want to be pinched," Julie said matter-of-factly.

"I'll think about it," was the only response Kelly would give. These ladies would get her arrested if she wasn't careful.

"Splendid!" the ladies responded, and Kelly started breakfast for the Southern belles.

* * * *

T. J.'s day started at seven a.m., fielding calls on his cell during the drive to his office in Charlotte. His superiors wanted this resolved as quickly as possible and kept out of the press. They did not want the bad publicity the situation could bring. T. J. thought it was fruitless because if it did turn out it was a military man, it would blow up across the newspapers anyway. By the time he got into his office, his mood was not a good one. He sat at his desk for an hour or two taking care of the day-to-day business of being in the military and being the man in charge. Then it was off to the county morgue to meet Danny and the medical examiner to go over Sherry Mayes.

Danny was already there when T. J. walked into the cold, sterile room. They were directed to exam room three where a short balding medical examiner was already autopsying the victim. He was playing oldies on a small CD player in the room while he had coffee and doughnuts sitting on his desk. Danny knew the squat little man by name and reputation of being thorough.

"God, Charlie. I always wonder how you can stand being in here and have food on the table with a dead body," Danny said.

T. J. wondered himself. He had seen death in some of the hardest conditions, 9/11 being one of them, but he never grew accustomed to the smell of death and hoped he never would. He thought that if he did, he wouldn't be human anymore.

The squat Charlie responded in a voice that sounded a little like a toad. "Good morning, Detective, who's your friend?"

"This is Lieutenant T. J. Chapel. He's in on the case."

"Didn't know that the murder had something to do with the military," said the examiner suddenly looking interested.

"It might not," T. J. replied. "We're just covering all of our bases."

The medical examiner looked from T. J., then to Danny. He was curious, T. J. knew, and he could see the curiosity about what was not being said. But he let it go. What did he care? He was just there to tell them how a person died. After that his job ended.

He continued his work as he talked. "It might explain a lot if the military is involved."

"What do you mean?" T. J. asked.

"Well, whoever did this has some training medical-wise. I was thinking doctor, maybe nurse, but now. . ." He let his words trail off.

"Come on, Charlie, what do you got?" Danny asked impatiently.

"Okay, this girl was not raped or sodomized, no tearing in any of the obvious places. She wasn't beaten or manhandled in any way."

"Probably killed the same day he took her," Danny murmured to himself. The medical examiner continued talking as if he had not interrupted.

"Her stomach contents were pasta and shrimp with some kind of sauce. I'm thinking Alfredo. Her drug screening came back clear of any toxins or drugs including alcohol, but here's the thing she was exsanguinated. Not by the usual way cutting the jugular or stabbing, he used a needle in her vein and let her bleed out. See here," he said, pointing to an obvious needle mark in her arm. "I'm thinking wide gauge needle and tubing of some sort."

Danny asked, "How much blood is in the human body?"

T. J. responded before the medical examiner could. "Ten pints."

"Very good, Lieutenant, you get a gold star," Charlie said looking pleased. "Anyway, he could just bleed her out into a container of some sort and dispose of it easy enough. This is what makes me think he has medical training. Look at the cut on her chest, perfect surgical cut, and the way he took the heart, not just lopped out like some maniac. He cut every artery precisely, as if he was harvesting the organ, and the stitches to close her chest perfect. He took time with them."

"What would the girl go through when he was bleeding her?"

"She would be dizzy, cold, lips and fingers would turn blue from loss of blood, unconsciousness from hypovolemic shock, then death soon after."

"So it was as if he was trying not to cause her pain in anyway," T. J. said. "I mean there could be quicker, more painful ways to do this?"

The medical examiner nodded in agreement.

Danny saw where T. J.'s thinking was going and added in his own thoughts as well. "Maybe it wasn't just about killing her. It was about the heart mainly and preserving the body. I mean her beauty. He didn't want her to look ugly."

"Seems that way to me," T. J. affirmed.

"Thanks, Charlie," Danny patted the old man's shoulders. "Anything else you come across, you let me know."

"You got it," he replied, turned his music back on, and continued his work.

On the way out Danny pulled out the file with the pictures of Sherry's body. "Look at this, T-man, how she is dressed and positioned. She looks like she is praying and dressed in all white like she is pure. I'm thinking he trussed her up like an angel or something. And Kelly saw him when he was fixing her up to the fence there."

T. J. had been thinking the same thing, but did not let on. His senses were telling him more than ever that this was a guy in the service, and he didn't like it one bit. "Did you get anything on the search for more murders in the area?"

"Yeah, well not around here. That would have been noticed right off, but we've found eight so far. Two in Oklahoma, two in New York, two in New Jersey, and two in Virginia in the last fifteen months."

"Plus the one here that makes nine."

Danny nodded. "Yup, so I'm thinking all the same guy, and he's not finished yet."

"Oh, I know he's not," T. J. said. His thoughts turned to Kelly Justine. He wondered if this bastard would try to go after her next since she had been there and had seen him. He could have the means to find her if he were military. He would keep an eye out without anyone knowing, especially her. He didn't need to scare her anymore by thinking someone was after her. It probably would be nothing anyway. He'd swing by her apartment after work sometime next week and see how she was doing, he decided, but till then, it was back to his office to take care of other matters that needed his attention.

* * * *

The days passed quickly for Kelly. Taking care of the ladies was definitely a full-time job. It was Friday again and eight days had passed since she saw Sherry Maye's body. She had spent the afternoon walking with Julie and Jenny and chatting over tea, which, she noticed, had been laced with a little bourbon by Jenny. When they decided they had to make fudge, she helped them in the kitchen and then played cards until dinnertime. After dinner, she made sure they took their medication for the evening and left them settled in front of the television watching the BET channel and discussing the dance moves of the girls in the videos.

She walked to the door, putting on her coat on the way, and called out, "I don't want you two trying anything you see on there!"

She got no response, and Kelly just smiled and closed the door. Just her luck she would find two old ladies with bad hips lying in bed after trying hip-hop moves. Her day ended late, after getting a ride home from her friend James and fending of his advances for the date she never got to the day before, a date she was somehow glad she missed. James was definitely not her type so she made a hasty goodbye and got out of the car. She was glad to be unlocking the door of her apartment. She stepped into the room and closed the door. Her shoes came off immediately, and she sighed as her toes sunk into the plush carpet. Her senses came back to the immediate surroundings. Something felt off. The hair on the back of her neck stood on end. Something felt wrong. Kelly walked around from room to room looking for anything out of place, but found nothing. She shrugged and let it go. Just nerves coming back making her edgy from the week before. Her next thoughts were food, and she padded barefoot to the cool tiles in the kitchen to make herself a meal. She took out the makings for a stir fry with vegetables and rice. She wasn't much of a meat eater so shrimp would go in with the veggies. As she made her meal, she poured a glass of wine and put on her favorite music, turning it up so it would erase the quietness of the empty rooms.

Kelly had been changing when she heard the knock on the door. *It couldn't be Abby,* she thought. *She would have just let herself in with her key.* She pulled on the shirt she had in her hands, went to the door, and looked through the peephole. Her mouth firmed into a tight line, and she opened the door to see the face of the rude lieutenant who she had talked to.

"Good evening, lieutenant." She said the words with formality that belied her real personality. T. J. looked at the woman standing in the door wearing pink shorts with lobsters printed all over them and a short T-shirt that said "I'm a brat" across the front with no shoes and her hair up in a ponytail again. The expression on her face was one of displeasure at seeing him. *He can't blame me, can he?* Kelly thought. He wasn't very gentle with her when he talked to her and dismissed her when he was done.

"Good evening, ma'am," he said. He took off his hat and held it in his hand.

"Kelly."

"Sorry, I mean, Kelly. I hope I'm not disturbing you."

"Just making dinner. What—wait a minute." Leaving him at the door, she turned around and used the remote to turn the music down which had turned to a reggae beat. As she turned, she knew he would see the run of the tattoos, designed like cheetah spots, that ran down her back.

"Now what do you want?"

Her tone was brisk and T. J. knew he had to smooth some ruffled feathers. "I was just checking to see if you were okay after last week."

"Why, Lieutenant, I didn't think you cared. After last week I would think you forgot me all together," she said sarcastically.

"Ma'am . . . Kelly, I was doing my job, and this situation is not easy for anyone involved."

Kelly sighed. "I guess you better come in."

He stepped into a room decorated in lush dark reds and cream. Peacock feathers sat in a vase and pillows were thrown everywhere on the floors and on the sofa. Pictures on the walls were of fairies sexily clad and erotic. One big portrait was of Kelly herself looking as if she was sitting in a mist, her hair loose down her back, and she looked like one of the fairies in the pictures. He felt a heat start inside him as he saw her now as more than a witness but something different. The apartment was unusual, it was different, and it was her.

"You can sit here. I'm in the kitchen getting my dinner," she said pointing to a stool that stood in front of the counter by the little kitchen.

"Smells good. Did you have something delivered?" The rumble in his stomach caused her to stare at him with an amused look and a raised eyebrow. He flushed boyishly. "I'm sorry, guess it smells better than I realized."

She laughed in that husky tone that T. J. liked. "To answer your first question, no delivery. I like to cook. I made this. Did you have dinner?"

"No, I haven't yet, ma'am—Kelly."

"Would you like a plate, lieutenant? Listen, do you have a name? I mean, I can't just go around calling you lieutenant all the time."

T. J.'s stomach rumbled again. "If it's no bother, and my name is T. J."

"It's not a bother, and T and J are letters, not a name. What does T. J. stand for?"

"I really don't like to say," he began but she waved him off with her hand as she set a plate of stir fry and rice in front of him.

"If I'm feeding you, you can tell me your name. Who am I going to tell? I doubt we run in the same circles."

The steaming food smelled heavenly, and when she set small sugar rolls next to his plate, the look on his face was like he could have kissed her fingers.

"Well?" she said.

"Well what?"

"Your name, soldier boy."

His face flushed as he picked up the fork she had set next to the plate. He muttered under his breath, "Taggert Julius."

She beamed a smile at him. "Well, that's a wonderful name. I'll just call you Taggert."

Around a mouth full of delicious food, he responded, "I'd rather you didn't."

"But I'd rather if I did," she replied. "So, Taggert, how's the food?"

"It's great. Wonderful. Thank you. I can't remember the last time I had a home-cooked meal, except when I go out to dinner."

"That's technically not home cooked, that's restaurant cooked. Do you get out often?"

He shook his head and said apologetically, "No, not really."

Kelly noted how he wolfed down his food, and he didn't seem to notice that she was piling more onto his plate.

"Why were you here again?" she asked.

"To check in to see if everything is okay," he replied. "When I was coming in, I noticed the complex was not that secure for a gated community, lots of trees and wooded areas." He took another bite of dinner before speaking again. "Plus, Danny—Detective Greywood—said you never called or anything to check in, so I decided to pay you a visit."

"That's very sweet of you. Everything is fine, but I felt strange when I came home this evening." She laughed it off. "Probably just nerves, but I have been feeling like someone's been in here for the past few days on and off."

He looked up quickly, instantly aware. "What do you mean? Is there anyone hanging around?"

"Like I said, it was nothing. It felt like someone was here, but I looked around, and nothing was different, nothing moved. Probably just me freaking myself out."

T. J. listened and nodded in agreement at her assessment, but she felt a tingle in the back of her neck at his intense stare. "How about if I come around every once in awhile to see if everything is okay?"

"Are you sure it's for me or just my cooking?" she teased.

"Maybe both." He smiled before finishing the meal on his plate.

* * * *

In the parking lot across from Kelly's building sat the blue car. The person inside watched. He saw the military officer go in forty-five minutes ago, and he had yet to come out. *There is no way I will lose my dove now!* he thought angrily. No one would keep her from him. In anger, he slapped his hands against the wheel of the car over and over again until the palm of his hand was sore and red. He stopped suddenly and again calmed his breathing. He was above this kind of outburst now. He would have his dove. He was sure of it. He kept watch on the lights of the apartment, his hands clenching and unclenching around a pair of white shoes on his lap.

He waited and waited until he saw the lieutenant leave the apartment. Oh yes, he knew it was a lieutenant. He knew the stripes well, and he already knew who the lieutenant was. He giggled to himself. *Lt. Taggert Julius Chapel of the*

United States Army. A good soldier who had gone up in the ranks quickly and who was very well trained. A pity if he got in the way, he would have to die. He was, after all, going up against a soon-to-be god. His ascension wasn't complete, but he was strong enough to take care of the lowly lieutenant. His smile grew wide as he thought of his power to take life as he chose. He felt the tingle low in his belly again, and he tried to ignore it, but the need grew. He just needed her to complete his transformation but one more for the pleasure of it. He would take delight in seeing life drain from her eyes. Her skin would be soft as he sliced into it, and her heart would still be warm as he cut it from her chest. Just a little playtime until he was ready to complete his destiny. He pulled out of the parking space and began to drive away. The lieutenant was gone, and his dove was still pure. He drove until he came to the west side of town where the street walkers and whores lived and worked. Not just any would do. He had standards that had to be met, even if she was not part of his grand plan.

He saw her then, young maybe eighteen or nineteen, no makeup on her face, but her beauty was visible. Her hair was braided and her skin seemed to glow under the ugly yellow light of the streets. *Seems a pity that she has to be a whore to survive,* he thought. He slowed the car to a stop in front of the woman in the tightest dress her small frame could fit into.

"Looking for something?" she asked with a small voice, trying to make it sound sexy, but he could tell she really didn't want to be there.

"Looks like I am," he responded giving her a wide smile. "How much for the package?"

"Fifty—I mean, seventy-five," she corrected hastily.

"Seventy-five, it is." He pulled out his wallet and began counting money. Her eyes grew wide as she saw the cash in his wallet, twenties, fifties, hundred dollar bills. He knew she had upped the price because of the car and she thought he could afford the extra money. That is why he counted each bill slowly, pulling the crisp new money between his fingertips for her to see. She had probably never seen so much in her life.

"Come on, get in, baby. I'll take you somewhere nice, and we can eat. You can take a bubble bath. I'll treat you really well," he promised. It didn't take much to convince her. She lived in squalor most of the time, lived on fast food. A chance to pretend she was something more, even if for just one night, sounded too good to pass up.

Chapter Four

T. J. was getting ready to leave Kelly's apartment. He had enjoyed her company and her cooking, and he found conversing with her fun and complex all at once. But he still had a bad feeling and decided to keep a closer eye on things because, if his suspicions were correct, she was now a target. She could jump from one topic to another without them being connected in any way. While talking to her, he also found out more about her life, her family, and the things she did in town for entertainment. All good information, if he was going to keep an eye on her. She had offered him tea because she was trying to quit coffee. He found that funny because with her upbeat personality, he didn't think she needed caffeine.

As he rose to leave, she got up to open the door for him and their bodies were inches apart. He felt the electricity between them, and his breath seemed to get trapped in his lungs. As Kelly looked up at him, he could see the definition of her face. Her hands crept up to touch his cheeks, but she caught herself before instinct moved her any further and smoothed her palms against her thighs. He felt disappointed at not feeling her touch.

The door behind them moved, jarring them out of the moment, and Abby walked in.

"Hey, girl, can you believe I'm just getting home? What's for—Oh, who's this?" Her voice sang out curiously.

"This is Lieutenant Chapel from the police station," Kelly replied.

"Oh, I see," was all Abby said.

T. J. felt Abby watching them, curious as to just what she had walked in on. "Taggert, this is Abby, my friend."

"Nice to meet you, ma'am." T. J. shook the hand of the slender little woman standing between he and Kelly. He looked at them and wondered how they were not mistaken for teenagers.

"Well, Lieutenant Taggert, what brings you around?" Abby asked.

"It's T. J., ma'am, and I am just checking in on Kelly to see if she was okay."

"Ah, well, that's good. She did have a scare. Which is it—Taggert or T. J.?"

"Well, both. Everyone calls me T. J. She just chose to call me Taggert for some reason."

Kelly added, "Well, it sounds better than T. J. People have names for a reason."

"Thank you for coming by, Taggert."

"It's no problem, if you see anything or think anything seems strange call me or Detective Greywood alright? And thank you for dinner."

"I'll do that, Lieutenant." Kelly gave him a little mock salute.

He smiled and shook his head as he closed the door. Walking to his car, he looked across the parking lot and saw a blue car with someone sitting behind the driver's seat, bent down and looking around for something. T. J. just figured the person was coming home late from work. He drove off thinking about Kelly Justine, what it would be like to kiss her, and what would have happened if her friend hadn't walked in. He pulled into the hidden driveway and sat in his car for moment. Silence surrounded him, and instead of the peace he usually felt, restlessness stirred inside him, and for a moment, he thought of the conversation and dinner he had with Kelly. Maybe his self-imposed solitude was not what he needed, but as his thoughts swirled, he heard the familiar barking of his longtime friend, and a massive body came barreling around the house up to the truck. When T. J. had found him wandering on the side of the busy interstate, he was just a puppy, scared, hungry, and skinny. T. J. had scooped him up with the intention of taking him to the animal shelter, but he ended up taking the pup that was all legs home with him. The pup was aptly named "Tank" because as he grew up he became a huge animal with thick muscles that rippled under his black coat.

"Hey, boy. Hey buddy," T. J. crooned to the dog.

As he got out of the car, the dog that had to weigh at least two hundred pounds tried to jump and put his big paws on T. J.'s chest. His breath whooshed out as he slammed back against the door of the truck.

"Down, Tank, now!" he commanded, and Tank automatically sat in front of his master with a sorry look on his face.

"Don't give me those eyes, and you know better," he scolded as he walked to the house.

Tank continued to sit by the truck until his master yelled, "Come!" Obediently, he trotted to his side. In his kitchen, T. J. went to his refrigerator and pulled out one of his favorite brands of beer. He crossed over to the sliding door that lead to his deck and sat down. With the night surrounding him like a blanket and the smell of the water in the air, he felt the familiar peace that he sought settle over him. He smiled and called himself crazy. *After one meal and good conversation with a woman, a witness no less, you're thinking you need more.* He shook his head and settled back into the deck chair, relaxing until his mind cleared and he knew he could sleep.

* * * *

The shrill ringing of the phone buzzed through the lieutenant's head early the next morning. He rolled over with a moan and looked at the offending machine with one eye. *It's Saturday,* he thought miserably. He was actually looking forward to maybe getting out on his boat today and pretending to fish, which entailed him lying and napping on deck all afternoon while holding a fishing rod.

"What," he growled into mouthpiece.

"T. J., it's Danny Greywood. You awake?"

"Now I am. What's up?"

"You'd better get down here to the Air Force base by the Charlotte Douglas Airport."

"Danny, I know where it is. What's this about?" T. J. was curt from having his sleep disrupted.

"We got another one, T-Man, and this time he left us a message."

T. J. was up and out of bed in seconds, dragging on his uniform that was always kept pressed in his closet.

"What message, Danny? Did he leave a note on the body?"

"Worse. He carved it into her forehead."

T. J. could hear Danny take a shuddering breath as if repulsed by what he was seeing. His loud swallow was a sound T. J. knew well, one to keep the bile rising in his throat down as best he could. He took the silence impatiently until he could no longer stand it even though it was only a few seconds.

"For God's sake, Danny, what does it say?" He yelled into the phone, startling his old friend out of his shocked horror.

"He carved her name into this girl's head. He carved 'Kelly' into her skin," Danny said.

"I am on my way. Get one of your units over to Kelly's apartment. Tell them not to go inside but to sit and wait until we get there. We don't need her more alarmed until we can give her more information."

"I'm doing my job, T. J.," Danny said sharply. "It will be done as soon as I get off the phone with you."

"I'm sorry, man, I'm sorry I didn't mean to imply—"

"Yeah, I know."

"She's his next target, Danny. We have to protect her."

"Yeah I know," was all Danny Greywood could say.

With that, T. J. hung up the phone and raced to his truck. This bastard was going to go down and go down hard, he swore to himself.

* * * *

There was a persistent knocking on the door of her apartment early Saturday morning, and Kelly climbed out of bed wearily. The last couple of days had been long, and she had been looking forward to sleeping in. Abby had left for a long weekend with her new boyfriend the night before so Kelly knew it couldn't be her. She crossed the room to the door and looked through the peephole. Her eyes met the uniform of a police officer, and she felt the warmth of sleep leave her for a cold chill. Something was wrong, she opened up the door immediately to the officer, and he just stood at the threshold surveying the room.

"Can I help you, officer? She asked.

"Yes, ma'am. Detective Greywood sent me to take you down to the station."

"Why? Is something wrong?"

"I'd better not say, ma'am. He said he would speak to you himself."

Kelly hesitated for a minute and then said, "Okay, I'll go get dressed. Give me a minute."

"Take your time, ma'am."

In her room, Kelly was pulling on her jeans when her cell phone rang. T. J. was on the other end.

"Kelly, are you okay?"

"Yes, Taggert, I'm fine. What's wrong?"

"We'll talk about it later. Just so you know, officers are going to be outside your apartment."

"I know, he's already here," Kelly replied. There was silence on the other end. "Taggert?

"Kelly," he said slowly, "what does this officer look like?"

"Oh, I don't know. I barely looked at him. He looked like any officer dressed in blue. I'm in my room getting dressed, why?" She heard the dread in Taggert's voice, and she felt a frisson of fear run down her spine.

"Listen to me carefully, Kelly. The officers could not be there already, not from uptown."

The chill Kelly felt was back, and it spread through her body until she was numb. She was listening to Taggert as if from a distance.

"Can you get out of the apartment?" she heard Taggert ask.

"No, I can't. It's too late, Taggert," she whispered. Leaving the person she thought was an officer standing at the door, she had walked into her bedroom. Now, as she turned and looked through the doorway, she saw him standing there, with a small smile on his face and cold green eyes. Cold green eyes she remembered. As she stared at him, the moment seemed to last forever, before instinct kicked in and he rushed toward the door. But Kelly got to it before he did, and she slammed it and turned the lock in one motion.

"Kelly! Kelly!" Taggert was yelling into the phone.

"I'm here, Taggert, I'm here." She was terrified.

"He's in the apartment. Oh, God! I'm locked in my bedroom. Oh, God! Oh, God!" She was panicking, knowing the locks on those doors were flimsy at best.

"Can you get out a window?"

"No," she squeaked out. "Too small." She looked around the room for a weapon, but her gaze fell on the big chest of drawers by the door. With her small frame pressed against it, she pushed and pushed against the heavy piece of furniture until it was in front of the door.

"Okay, the cops are almost there."

From beyond the locked door, she could hear the intruder's soft voice talking to her crawling along her skin like cold fingers.

"My beautiful dove, there is something wonderful in store for you don't you know? Let me show——"

* * * *

Taggert heard her scream, "Leave me alone!" His heart jumped at the sound of her voice. He had made a call to Danny while keeping the call on three-way, to hurry the squad car to her place, only to hear there was a bad accident on the highway and they had to take a longer route. Danny was on his way, leaving the crime scene in the hands of the CSI unit and his partner.

The voice on the other side of the door became cold as he spoke to his dove, he knew that time was running out and he could be caught. "Open the door, Kelly, you are holding back destiny, our destiny."

When he got no response, his anger took over and be banged his shoulder against the door trying to break it down. It moved a little but the barrier she had put in front of it held firm.

"You won't be able to get away from me. It's fate, Kelly, you'll see."

Still no response and in a last fit of fury he tried to kick the door in. T. J. heard loud bangs and Kelly screaming. It echoed in his head as the line went dead. He drove like a maniac, breaking the speed limits trying to get to her. He pulled into the parking lot in front of her building and did not bother turning off his car. He could hear sirens coming his way, but they were not there yet. He had to go in. With his gun drawn, he cautiously came up to the door, which was wide open. No neighbors were around, and he assumed it was because of the time of morning or that people just didn't want to be involved. He swung inside quickly and moved into a low stance so he could take out his target if necessary, but saw no one. T. J. checked the rest of the apartment before going to the bed room door; he could hear her quietly sobbing at the other side.

"Kelly," he said. At the sound of her name, she began to scream again.

"No, no it's me. T. J.—Taggert. It's okay now. He's gone."

"Gone? Are you sure?" She hiccupped after a sob.

"Yes. Open the door."

"I c-can't," she wailed.

"Why not?"

"It's too heavy to move!" And with that, she broke down crying again.

He sighed and said to her through the closed door, "Stand back."

He kicked the door and the lock broke easily. He looked at it with disgust, knowing that if she hadn't barred it, he would have gotten her. With a few more good shoves he had it moved enough that he could squeeze through. She was sitting on the floor with her arms wrapped around her knees. He looked at the large chest of drawers and wondered how she had found the strength to move it, but then his focus was on her. He moved to her, and when he put his hand on her shoulder, she shrank away from his touch, making him want to smash the bastard's face in with his bare fist.

"Ssshh, baby, it's me, T. J. It's okay now. You're safe."

She lifted her head from her knees and looked at him with tears flowing down her face. Her hair was wild, almost out of its familiar ponytail, and she launched herself into his arms. He pulled her onto his lap and sat there rocking her, giving her comfort, letting her cry away all her fear. That was how Danny and the other officers found them as they came rushing in.

"Is she okay, hurt in any way?" Danny asked. His gun was still drawn, and he looked around the room. The other officers knowing the job well began to process her apartment looking for fingerprints.

"No, she's fine. She barred herself in the room."

"With that thing?" Danny asked dubiously looking at the big antique drawers.

"Yeah. How she managed it, I don't know."

"Yeah, well, it saved her life."

"I'm still in the room, you know." Her voice came muffled from T. J.'s shoulder.

"How did you move that monstrous thing?" T. J. asked Kelly as she lifted her head from his neck. He loved how she smelled, like spices and vanilla. He wanted to keep her face pressed against his warm skin. He knew it would be so easy to give in to the temptation, so when she moved away from him and sat on the edge of her bed, he let her.

"I don't know how I did it. I just put my back against it and pushed. I knew I had to, if not he could get me. I just knew that if I didn't . . ." Her voice trailed off, and she shuddered.

T. J. put his arm around her looked up at Danny, seeing a big grin on his face, though he said nothing.

"She can't stay here." T. J. was the first to put the statement out there.

"I can stay upstairs with my friend Abby."

"No, you can't. He'd know, and then both of you would be in harm's way."

"We could put her in a safehouse."

"No we can't."

"He found out who she is, where she lives. He's getting the information from somewhere."

Danny bristled, instantly defensive. "Now wait a damn minute, T. J., there is no leak on my team, and if you are implying that there is, we are going to have a problem."

"I wasn't implying there was. Just that he knows how to get at the information," T. J. retorted.

"Okay, safehouse is out. What do you suggest?"

"How about a hotel with guards?" T. J. posed the question.

They both shook their heads in denial to that one. There were too many variables and no way to cover all the bases for her protection. Then Danny came with one last idea, but T. J. balked at it even though he knew that it was probably the best option.

"How about you take her home with you?" he asked

Kelly, who was sitting quietly and barely listening to the exchange, popped up immediately to protest the idea, but T. J. beat her to it.

"No way, Danny. She can't come home with me. It's my house for goodness sake, and I like my privacy."

"I don't want to go to his house. Can't I just go with the hotel idea?" Kelly piped in.

"No, it won't work, and, T. J., you know it's the best idea. Your house is secluded, hardly anyone knows you live out there, you have an alarm system, you know the area, and we can keep a patrol car out there."

He knew Danny was right but made a last ditch effort to find another solution. "Can't we think of something else?"

"Well, geez, I don't want to intrude on his fortress of solitude," Kelly said sarcastically. "I'll just stay here and die quietly so as not to disturb him." That comment got her a sharp look from T. J.

"It's the best we got. You got any better ideas?" T. J. shook his head no and sighed heavily. He gave in to the idea with silent disapproval. He didn't have to like it, did he?

"Get some stuff together. We're going to get you out of here," T. J. said impatiently.

"Well, someone has to tell Abby when she comes home. She went away for the weekend, and she'll worry. And the leasing office will need to know what happened so they can fix the door, my job—I have to go to work and explain to the ladies."

"You work?"

"Why, Taggert, does it look like I have a money tree growing in a pot of soil out there? Of course I work," she snapped.

"Listen you—" T. J. began, his temper starting to simmer.

"Who are you calling *you*? I have a bloody name, Taggert!" She spat his name out like it was a bad-tasting medicine.

"Okay, okay," Danny jumped in. "We'll take care of everything one at a time. I'll go up to the office and fill them in a little. I'll tell them you had a break-in and you will need your door fixed and bolted. Plus give the keys to your friend upstairs until you come back from extended vacation. Is your rent paid up?"

She nodded. "Until the end of the year, I like to keep ahead."

Danny went on. "Good. You can call your friend when she comes home. Don't use your cell phone, use T. J.'s home line. Go call your boss and tell them you had a family emergency and you need a couple of weeks off, and then get packed to leave."

She nodded again, placed her hand on Danny's shoulder, and simply said a thank you as she passed him to do as she was told, her eyes shooting daggers at T. J. as she did.

An hour later, she was ready. He grumbled to himself about her luggage— so far, three big suitcases, one of which felt like it weighed a ton, and two smaller bags. He and Danny had already coordinated their plan. There would be a patrol car outside his place, and it would change every twelve hours. The officers would come to his door and let him know the change had been made. Danny left with a handshake and a call of good luck. He would also be going up to T. J.'s house regularly to keep an eye on things. While they searched for a killer, he would be her protector. She got into the tall truck as gracefully as possible in heels and jeans and sat there looking out the window silently as he drove.

"So what's in all those heavy bags, carting bricks?" he asked jokingly, trying to bring her out of her silence.

"Listen, I know you don't want me at your house, and you are being forced to, so you don't have to make conversation. I'll stay out of your way," she snapped.

He sighed, took her hand from her lap, and held it. "It's going to be okay, Kelly. I promise." With her gaze still focused out the window, she said nothing in return, but her fingers twined with his as he drove.

Chapter Five

The drive to Lake Norman was about an hour, and every mile farther from the troubles in Charlotte the tightness in Kelly's chest lessened. She was unhappy about leaving her home and her need for sanctuary, but she felt safer with Taggert and, even though she didn't want to admit it, a little excited to be in his home and close to him.

"We're coming up to the house." Her eyes widened as he made a turn into the driveway that led up to a wonderfully designed house. The house, done in a cabin style but so much more, was inviting, with its rich dark colored wood and the wraparound veranda with the beautifully crafted rocking chairs that called to one to sit and relax. The bottom floor was all windows, giving a sophistication to the cabin feel, and the landscaped lawn and flowers, and the hanging plants all over the house. Kelly fell in love with it instantly.

"You live here?" she asked with a surprised voice.

His blue eyes sparkling with humor, he raised an eyebrow at her. "You were expecting a one room shack with an outhouse?"

"Well, no," she began. "But definitely this is beautiful. Did you design it yourself?"

"My thought, my cousin's creation."

"I think it's spectacular."

She saw the pleased grin on his face. "Wait until you see the inside."

He was right. She loved the look and the warmth of his décor—two big overstuffed sofas in a dark beige color, mahogany tables, and more plants—but she fell in love with his kitchen, a huge open space with stainless steel appliances and marble counters. It was designed to create culinary magic, and Kelly wanted to take it home with her when she left. She looked around at everything, and she hoped that Taggert had no feelings of invasion of space he thought he would have.

"I'll go get your bags, and I'll take you upstairs to get settled."

A loud bark came from the back, and Kelly saw a huge black figure barreling toward her. With a loud shriek, she turned and tried to run but was too late. The big animal jumped up and put its paws on her shoulders, its weight sending them both crashing to the floor. Kelly felt her breath whoosh out of her body and then the dog drowned her with slobbering licks all over her face.

"Get off, Tank! Bad boy!" Taggert practically had to pull the happy dog off her. "Are you okay? Are you hurt?"

She lay there, trying to catch her breath. "What is that thing?"

"*He's* not a thing. This is Tank. He's a good doggy, aren't you, boy?" He rubbed the dog's stomach, which caused the effect of his tail thumping loudly on the floor.

"That's not a dog, that's some sort of prehistoric animal!"

"He's a mastiff, and he's friendly. Come on, pet him, and let him apologize."

She scooted on her knees and petted the huge slobbering dog cautiously. She looked at the huge face, which looked like it was smiling, and felt a little more comfortable. As she petted him, she remembered the movie *Cujo* and hoped he didn't have any intention of biting off her arm.

"Okay, let's get back to getting you settled upstairs."

Quickly, Kelly got up and stepped in front of Taggert. "Before you go, I wanted to say thank you for doing this," she added hastily. "I want you to know I won't be a bother and I'll help out with laundry, cleaning anything you need to be done."

She was standing too close, she could feel the warmth radiating off his body and smell his aftershave.

"You don't need to do anything. Just know you're safe here, okay?" he replied softly.

Her hand went to his face this time and she could feel the beginning of his five-o'clock shadow coming in. She caressed it slowly and he closed his eyes in pleasure at her touch. "Thank You," she said simply. Kelly could tell instinctively they were going to have a hard time keeping their hands off each other.

"Let's get your things," he sad gruffly.

Upstairs was just as beautiful as downstairs. The room she was to stay in was a rich cream color. A big sleigh bed sat in the middle of the room with a soft plush chair by a gorgeous bay window that looked out to the lake. The water lapped gently, and the rays of the sun reflected off the surface. She turned when she heard him open the door; his hands full with her luggage and the straps of her bags across his chest. Her mouth turned to wide smile as he stumbled across the threshold of the bedroom.

"What do you have in here?" he asked as he dropped one of the bags on the floor with a thud.

She went over to help him. "My essentials. Makeup, clothes, books, and that one case there has my shoes."

"How many damn pairs of shoes do you need?"

"Hey! There are shoes in there for every style I am going for. Just because I am in hiding doesn't mean I'm going to be wearing sneakers everyday."

He looked at her and broke into a rich full laughter at her expression. The sound flowed over her, and she felt goosebumps along her arms. He was so beautiful when he was laughing. Kelly was a woman who followed her impulses, and this time was no different. She crossed to where he stood still trying to control his laughter. Her gaze caught his, and when she took his face in her hands, the laughter stopped. A different aura filled the air, her lips touched his, and she was lost. The kiss was soft and sweet. She nibbled his lips, tasting him and feeling the texture of his lips. When it ended, Kelly slowly opened her eyes to the intense blue of Taggert's eyes.

"I had to do that," she said. "I just followed my instincts and I'm glad I did."

"Now I'm going to follow my instinct." He growled at her. Grabbing her shoulders, he pushed her against the cream-colored wall, and then he plundered her mouth. Gone were the soft sweet kisses, replaced with molten hot sexuality. His mouth was hard on hers, his tongue sweeping into her mouth to take her taste. She moaned in pleasure, which spurred him on more. Taggert buried his hand in her hair, and the band holding her hair in the ponytail fell to the floor, freeing her hair. He moaned low in his throat and fisted his hands in the thick tresses. Then he pulled away and tried to regain his control and his breathing. She could envision him taking her right there on that bed, but she knew he was supposed to keep her safe, not take advantage her. He was too honorable to do that no matter how he wanted her. Kelly stood there against the wall, trying to comprehend what had just happened. She had initiated the kiss, but this was so much more than she had expected. Her bones felt like jelly, and she thought if she tried to walk, she would just crumple to the floor. She had never felt anything like that before. The heat that had gone through her body still surged under the surface, and she wanted more of him of his touch.

"I'm sorry," he said.

She looked at him and she could see the desire in his eyes. "I'm not, Taggert," she replied. "That kiss alone was incredible."

"Do you always speak so freely, like everything is so simple?"

"As I see it, you want me, I want you. What is more simple than that?"

"You have a tongue ring. I felt it when I kissed you."

"Yup," was her simple reply.

He shook his head and combed his fingers through his hair. "Well, for one, you're a witness to a serious crime, you're being stalked, and I'm supposed to be your protector."

"Uh-huh."

"It's wrong, it goes against policy. I can't go around sleeping with a witness."

"Who said we'd be sleeping?" she said with a big smile.

"You're nuts."

"Okay. I can see you need time to think about this so we'll put it off for now."

"Gee, thanks, I feel so safe now," he replied sarcastically. "I'm the guy, remember?"

"Yes, and I am a woman who knows what she wants and goes with it. We are going to have each other, and it's going to be hot and intense. I'll figure out the rest after we get to that point."

"Don't I have a say?"

But Kelly, feeling steadier on her feet, wasn't even listening. She had begun to unpack her things and was humming to herself.

"You live in your own reality. You'll send me to the nut house, if I'm not careful." Taggert sighed as though it was useless to attempt to finish the conversation and left the room, closing the door behind him.

As he closed he door, Kelly smiled to herself. *Maybe this will be a little more interesting than I thought.*

* * * *

An hour later, Kelly came down the stairs to see what she could find for a late lunch in the kitchen. It was already after one, and since she didn't get any breakfast, her stomach was complaining, letting its hunger be known. There was no sign of Taggert when she got to the kitchen, but when she heard the barking of his huge dog, she looked out the window to the backyard and saw him playing with Tank. He threw an obviously well-used ball, and Tank snapped it out of the air and brought it back to him. *Okay, maybe not like Cujo,* she thought, but she still would not be getting between him and his food. Food sent her mind back to the task at hand. She opened the stainless steel refrigerator and saw what she expected—two frozen pizzas, some old leftover Chinese food, a case of Michelob beer, and, from the smell, old milk or cheese. She wrinkled her nose in disgust and closed the door. *Okay,* she thought to herself making her way to the sliding doors that led to the backyard. Kelly could see by the smoldering look in his eyes that his temperature rose a few degrees when he saw her standing there in pink shorts, a little lace halter top, and bare feet.

He called across the expanse of lawn to her. "Something you need, island girl?"

"Yes, as a matter of fact, I do. You have nothing in your refrigerator to eat. I think you are conducting a few experiments, but no food. We need to go shopping."

He took his time walking over to her. "There's cereal in the pantry and some tuna and stuff."

Kelly gave him a look of absolute amazement. "You're kidding, right? You have no milk for cereal anyway. You're making penicillin in there, and what am I supposed to make tuna with no bread, no mayo, or no onions?"

"Well, we can't go shopping. You're supposed to be invisible right now."

"Listen, I'm starved."

"Make me a list. I'll pick up some stuff from the store."

"I'm picky. I need to go." Kelly could see Taggert's frustration building so she tried another tactic. Her mother always said you can catch more flies with honey that with vinegar. "Taggert," she began with a gentle sexy voice, her accent a little thicker and entirely British. "We need to eat, and I'm sure you're hungry. I'd love to cook in your kitchen. How does little red potatoes mashed with a little cheese, chives, and onions, sautéed pork chops with mushrooms, and steamed asparagus sound for dinner?"

"It's after two now. What's for lunch?"

We'll get some sliced bread and some cold cuts, and I'll make sandwiches to tie us over until dinner. I'll even make brownies for dessert and fresh bread for tomorrow."

"You bake bread and brownies?" he asked dubiously.

She could feel his resolve slipping. "From scratch," she said in a staged whisper.

"Okay, it's a deal, but we're in and we're out." At her raised eyebrows, he got her double-meaning and said, "Of the supermarket."

She laughed. "So we're ready to go?"

"Don't you have to change?" he asked looking at the expanse of skin her shorts and top exposed.

"Nope," and off she went around the house to get into his truck. Seeing her move to the truck, the dog decided he wasn't going to be left behind, jumped into the flatbed, and settled in for the ride.

"I guess he's coming along too," Taggert muttered while he climbed into the cab of the Dodge truck. Kelly was already settled and seatbelted in with her sunglasses and a smile on her face. The ride to the Harris Teeter supermarket was about fifteen minutes, and in that time, Kelly decided that the only radio station he had programmed in the truck was country music. After the fifth song about someone losing a love and their dog, she decided to flip through the channels only to have her hand slapped.

"Hey, what's that for?"

"Nobody messes with my radio."

"Well, if you didn't just have music about someone's horse dying or broken hearts for the last ten minutes, I wouldn't have to change it!" Kelly tried to switch it again only to have her hand slapped again.

"Now, look you . . ."

Before she could get the rest of the sentence out that would have included some kind of insult, his telephone rang cutting her off. He checked the number and with his finger to his lips directed her to shush. Kelly slouched back against the seat of the truck and pouted, miffed she was foiled by a cell phone.

"Hey, Danny, what's the word?"

Detective Greywood's name perked up her ears, and she decided to listen to the conversation. *Maybe they caught the guy, and I'm safe.* Unlikely, but she was allowed to hope. But all Taggert's responses were "uh-huh," "okay", "yes," or "no," so she had no clue to what was being said on the other line.

"Okay, well, keep me informed." The phone clicked as he hung up and continued to drive in silence.

"Well?"

"Well what?"

"What did the detective have to say? Did they catch him?"

"No, they didn't."

"What was that about, Taggert? What's wrong? I'm involved, way involved, I have a right to know. You know I'm right. Better I find out from you than the eleven o' clock news."

He sighed. "There was another murder last night."

She stared at him shocked, terrified and horrified all at once. Her voice came as a whisper. "When?"

"We don't have an exact time, but we think while the police were out at that crime scene, he intercepted the call to protect you and went after you this morning."

"But how could he do that, how could he know? Why would he kill again if he wants me?"

"We're thinking he couldn't control the urge. It's not just killing for him, Kelly. It's personal, plus he wanted to send a message to us."

"What message? What aren't you telling me?" Kelly demanded to know.

"He carved your name in her forehead."

"Oh my God, no! That girl, that girl she's dead because of me." Her body shook and she buried her face in her hands.

"Listen to me, Kelly Justine, this is not your fault! This guy was sick long before you saw him, and he's done this before. Don't you dare blame yourself for his sickness."

Kelly looked over at Taggert and could see the controlled fury in him in how his hands gripped the steering wheel until his knuckles were white. She was scared, but she knew she needed to be strong because if she weren't, she would not be able to overcome this terror in her life. Taggert seemed to notice the change in her demeanor, the way she firmed her back and set her mouth in determination.

"Good girl," he said, and then he took her hand again in support.

By the time they got to the Harris Teeter supermarket, her mood had changed from bubbly and happy to quiet. She was inside her own head. Taggert, as if sensing her thoughts, knew it did no good for her to think about it too much. He tried to turn her thoughts to food and the reason why they were out. The looks she got from the older ladies amused her. She was unlike the people they were used to in this neighborhood. The looks from the men

old and young alike had Taggert muttering about wanting to punch their lights
out, which made Kelly smile.

"Don't know why we're here," he grumbled good-naturedly. "We could
have opened a can of baked beans and made some mac and cheese."

Horrified, Kelly looked at him. "You're kidding, right?"
And when he shook his head solemnly, she shook her head in disappointment.
"You're a hopeless cause, Taggert. I'll show you what real food is."

* * * *

She started on a mission to tempt his taste buds. One full cart and a hundred
fifty dollars later, they walked out of the supermarket. T. J. wondered where
all the groceries were going, and while he drove, he listened to Kelly's excited
chatter about getting back to his kitchen and starting to create.

They got home in record time. T. J. was having a good time, and he was
surprised yet again that he didn't feel invaded by her presence. He even got a
laugh out of her when he kept slapping at her hand when she fiddled with his
radio during the drive home. They unloaded the food, and he helped her to
put it away.

"Now, get out." She shooed him away from the kitchen.

"But my sandwich—" he started. After doing all that at the grocery store,
his stomach rumbled for nourishment.

"You'll have one in a few. Just let me get some preparations done in here
for dinner."

"Okay, I'm going to go to my office and get some work done. I need to
catch up on some paperwork."

"Taggert, why are you protecting me? I mean they must give you a lot of
responsibilities in the military, why are you doing both? The cops could watch
me."

"Well, for one, the military has a vested interest in this case, and two, I'm
good at both, so don't worry."

"Okay." She turned and went into the kitchen.

T. J. watched her leave, the way her bottom swayed as she walked, and
how her hair bounced. He wanted to sink his fingers into those tresses once
again. He then turned and closed the door to his office. He had some soldier's
profiles from all the sites of the previous murders to go through. These were
guys who had transferred in and out of those military installations at or around

the time the killing happened. He was looking for a link, one person that was there every time and at every place.

Thirty minutes later, Kelly walked in with a sandwich and a drink, placed them on his desk, and left as quietly as she came in. He barely looked up from the papers he was engrossed in, but the smell of something delicious had him reaching over and grabbing half the meaty sandwich. On his first bite, he closed his eyes with pleasure. *She even makes a good sandwich,* he thought as he took a second bite. His mouth filled with different kinds of meat and cheese melted on top, of the hot pickles mixed, of the lettuce and tomato. And how did she know he loved extra mayo on his bread? *If she keeps this up, I'll have to marry her,* he thought again with a big smile on his face. He polished off the rest of his meal and went back to work.

* * * *

He fumed at the thought of losing his dove. She was barring him from victory! He bit his finger in an act of childish tantrum. With tears streaming down his face, he rolled and floundered around on the bed and acted out his anger. With his breathing harsh and tears on his cheeks, he lay there after his episode and tried to calm down. It was just a set back. He would find her. They could not hide her so well that she would be out of his sight for long. It was time for him to go and find his precious dove. He dressed in his uniform making sure he looked his best, always to look his best like he was taught. He walked over to the corner of the room and bent down.

She could not be more than eighteen. After his incomplete mission of capturing his dove, he'd picked her up off the side of the road hitchhiking toward Greensboro. He had convinced her to come with him for a meal before he took her to her destination. Now she was tied up in the corner of his sanctuary, her eyes wide and frightened, just how he liked them.

This one was pretty. In the days since he took her from the side of the street, he had used her body. Even gods have needs. He would take her body, but not her heart. She would be the one to pay for his dove's transgressions. He kissed her on the head, stroking her blonde hair. It wasn't thick like Kelly's, but she would do.

"I'll be back soon then we can play," he said softly before walking out the door. He made sure it locked behind him.

The waif was in the corner of the dark room. Her gaze went wildly around the room, settling on the jars that were placed on individual pedestals, each filled with some kind of liquid and containing a heart. She closed her eyes to the horror and shrank into the corner trying to fade away or blend into the walls to escape him. With a kind of whimper that sounded like an animal caught in a trap, she tried to scream behind the gag in her mouth.

He came back later with a big smile on his face. He'd gotten what he needed from the willing police woman where the big lummox detective worked. It didn't take long to convince her to sneak a peek at his files for him. A lie about Detective Greywood withholding information from the military, a little flirting, and a promise of dinner later in the week was all it took. He sat in the chair where he was worshipped and looked around his sanctuary every heart beating just for him, and he ate the meal he had brought in with gusto. *He has taken her to his house,* he thought, and his smile faded. Kelly was a beautiful woman, and he did not want to think of the lieutenant touching his dove or soiling her in any way. He lost his appetite and angrily threw the rest of his food against the wall.

Waking the girl in the corner, her eyes popped open filled with terror as he came over to her. He pulled her to her feet dragged her across the room to the bed. He hand cuffed each arm and leg to the bedpost and foot rails, leaving her spread eagle. He stripped off his clothes quickly and climbed onto her, taking her savagely before stabbing her to death. There was no tenderness to his actions. He wanted to inflict pain. He thought of Kelly and the lieutenant, how he might touch her, his dove, and he carved at her body. The girl's eyes were dead long ago, but he still had his hands in her warm blood, taking her heart out and then just leaving it in the dead corpse. *This one will be a message,* he thought, and this time he would not fail at getting his prize. He cleaned up the mess he had created with food and blood, thankful that he was trained how to do so. Then he took the body out to the beat-up car he had bought for a few hundred dollars and left it where it would be found, to show his anger and how a god dispensed vengeance.

Chapter Six

T. J. was in bed, but he was not asleep. He was thinking about the woman down the hall in his guest room. She was probably sleeping or reading one of those many books that he'd trudged up the stairs. *One of those bags was actually full of books,* he thought with a smile. It had been a week since she came to stay with him, and so far, everything was working out. She was a bit messy, leaving her stuff wherever her hand left them, which had caused a few little spats with him being a guy who likes everything in its place. The spats ended with Kelly calling him uptight. She made wonderful meals and homemade desserts, and he swore his waist line was getting bigger. She was a remarkable cook, keeping to her promise that first Saturday with the sandwich. That evening, as she said, she made him pork chops and mashed potatoes. When he first saw them with the little bits of red skin mixed in, he had been doubtful to eat it.

"It's better that way. If you can eat potato skins, you can eat this," she had said to him.

The smell had made his mouth water, and when he'd taken the first bite, he had closed his eyes in delight. The taste of her potatoes was so different. Cheese and some other spices made them full-bodied and creamy. The pork chops were tender and spicy yet with a tang he didn't recognize. She'd even made him red velvet cake for dessert, and after three pieces, he was stuffed. He'd helped her clean up the kitchen after dinner, and then they sat in the living room together. He watched TV and she sat by the window to read.

T. J. frowned as he remembered looking over at her and her mind was not engrossed in a book. Across her lap, it had lain opened to an unread page, and she had been staring out into the night and to the lake. He'd known she was thinking about the past couple of days how her life turned upside down so quickly. Then she had abruptly got up and announced she was going to bed. With a quick goodnight, she had run up the stairs, and he heard the bedroom door close behind her. Soon, after days of nothing happening, she had started to feel more secure, but every time the phone rang, she jumped. But now, he could see her visibly relaxing, even going for walks down by the lake.

The tension was there also. Whenever they stood too close or bumped into each other, he wanted to grab her and kiss the hell out of her as he had done in her bedroom. It always ended the same way, though, with him muttering excuses and Kelly smiling at him, saying sweetly, "It's okay, Taggert." The sexy British accent was driving him crazy as well. He wondered if it changed when she was hot and ready in the midst of passion.

Now it was Saturday again, and he lay in bed in his pajama bottoms, looking up at his ceiling thinking about this woman who had made an impression on him, even if he didn't want her to. T. J. wanted her, could feel it every time she looked at him with those chocolate eyes. At the thought of her skin, the color of mocha, another thought ran through his head. *Does she taste as good as she smells?* He shook his head trying to dislodge the intimate thoughts that were running through his mind. Tank's head popped up from the bottom of his bed with his ears perked up. T. J. had forgotten the lummox of a dog was sleeping there.

"What did ya hear, boy?" he asked as he propped up on his elbow to look at the dog.

Then he heard it too, a scream from Kelly's room. He heard it again, was out of bed in a flash, and was running down the hallway with bare feet. He threw the door open to her room and saw her sitting on her bed, her eyes wide and staring. She screamed again, still caught in the dream plaguing her. He sat on the bed and took her by the shoulder. She fought him, fought his touch as if he was the unknown demon that chased her in her dreams.

"Kelly, Kelly!" he said more firmly, giving her a little shake. "It's me T. J., It's Taggert, honey. Wake up now, it's okay!"

He caught her flailing arms and held her close until her struggles ceased. He watched her eyes flutter as she fought her way to reality.

"Taggert?" she whispered. "Oh God, oh God, oh God."

"Yes, baby, it's me. It's okay, you're safe."

She shivered and held on tighter to him.

"Bad dream, huh?" he asked gently.

"It was awful. He had me, Taggert, and he was going to kill me like he did

Sherry and all the other girls." She looked up at him, her eyes filled with terror. "I'm going to die, aren't I? You won't be able to stop him, and he'll kill me, won't he?"

He pulled her away from him and said harshly. "That won't happen you hear me? I won't *ever* let that happen." He pulled her into his arms once again and squeezed her tight still muttering. "I won't let him get to you, I swear I won't."

They sat there holding each other, sharing comfort, his arms rubbing against her back then his hand slowed and then stilled as he felt a whole lot of skin.

"Uh, Kelly?"

"Hmm?"

"What are you wearing?"

She was almost nude, and her voice held humor as she spoke. "Bra and panties. That's what I always sleep in."

He pushed her away and sat back. He had been so concerned about her safety and welfare that he hadn't notice the purple bra. He certainly did now, and how her hips curved into the tops of bikini panties he could just make out under the sheet.

"Why aren't you wearing clothes?"

"Hey," she said defensively, "why aren't you?"

"I'm wearing clothes."

Looking at his pajamas bottoms, she retorted, "Not much more than I am. M&M print?"

"I was concerned, and leave my pajamas out of it."

Kelly looked at him, and a snicker slipped past her lips. She pressed her hand against her mouth as he narrowed his eyes on her dangerously.

"Don't you dare laugh at me," he growled.

She let loose, laughing uproariously at the military lieutenant wearing M&M-print pajama bottoms. His eyes narrowed before he lunged at her and pinned her to the bed with his body, her hands pinned above her head.

"Now, wait a minute," she began, her eyes filled with mirth.

"You're in trouble now. Laugh at me, will ya?"

"Hey, it was funny, and what are you going to do anyway? You can't use your hands to tickle me so . . ." She stuck her tongue out at him, and again, he caught a glance of the silver ring that went through it.

"Your tongue is pierced," he said.

"No flies on you. I thought we established that last kiss." She laughed softly.

"Why?"

"Why not?"

"Okay, you have your tongue pierced, spots tattooed on your back. Any other things I should know about, any other piercings, tattoos?"

"A couple more of both."

"Where?"

She looked down, and his gaze followed. Above her breast was a picture of a little devil with a pitchfork and the words "Hot Stuff" written under it. Through the flimsy lace of her bra, he saw the sliver glint of rings in her nipples.

"The others you'll have to find," she said in a sexy whisper.

"I'm telling you right now you're not the type of woman that I'd fall for."

"Really? What type do you fall for?"

"Not your type."

"And what is my type, Taggert? A tattooed woman with piercings who knows how to have fun and enjoys herself?"

"Yes, no. I mean you probably go to clubs and dance and drink and stuff. You've changed your hair color twice since I've met you, and that's only in a little over a week. I like to stay home and watch the History Channel and sit on my deck with my dog."

"I didn't think you noticed my hair, that's so sweet," she cooed.

"I noticed."

"You ever think that maybe the kind of girl I am would loosen you up more, so you can let your proverbial hair down?"

"My hair is fine where it's at."

"My hair suit my moods, I'll have you know. I will point out that we are having this conversation on a bed with you on top of me so there's some spice in you, Taggert." She arched an eyebrow and stared at him waiting for his response.

His response was to take her lips in a hot kiss. With his body pressed against hers, his mouth devoured hers, and she responded matching his kiss with her fire. He could feel his body melting from the heat that they made. Just like before it was like a flash fire that went straight through him. His hands still had hers captured above her head. She was restrained, exposed, vulnerable, and open to him. Their tongues mated and dueled from his mouth to hers.

What she couldn't do with her hands, she did with her lips, making sure he knew that she wanted him right there, right now. He tore his mouth away from hers. T. J. wanted to immerse himself in her taste. Kissing her was not enough; he needed more. His mouth traveled down to the curve of her neck, and he kissed and licked at the sensitive skin before biting it softly.

Kelly arched in pleasure as she felt his teeth against her skin "Taggert, more."

Her sexy voice low husky, and that accent drove him on. He moved his lips down to her breast suckling her through the thin fabric of her bra. He could feel her nipple in his mouth beaded hard and the cool metal of the ring that ran through it. It was like a bolt of electricity between her thighs and her body bucked beneath him in ecstasy. He used his thighs to part her legs and settle between them. Kelly's hip rose and pressed the most intimate part of her against his already aroused body. She moaned his name in pleasure again, and somewhere, an inner voice made him stop. *This is wrong.* He couldn't do this. She was a witness and scared. He couldn't take advantage of her like that. He let go of her hands and she instantly stroked his back. Her hands were soft and felt like fire against his skin. T. J. could feel his resolve slipping, and he moved away quickly, levering himself off her and backing away to the doorway.

Their breathing was the only sound in the quiet room as they looked at each other.

"Why did you stop?" she asked softly.

"It's not right, Kelly. I can't do this."

Kelly's gaze met him standing there, and a chill settled where there had once been a fire growing inside her. Her voice was cold and her eyes angry. "I seem good enough to roll around with, but like you said I'm not your type, right?"

"Don't worry, Taggert, I'm not a slut. Believe it or not, even though I go out and I party with my friends, and I like to dance and have fun, and I dress like I do, it doesn't mean that I sleep around. I'm very selective about my bedmates. I know when I'm wanted. You won't have to worry about me touching you anymore. You're obviously not interested."

She was getting the wrong impression. T. J. could feel the want deep to his core. He didn't want her to think she turned him off. It just wasn't right. His job was to protect her.

"It's not like that, Kelly, I—"

"It's fine, lieutenant, you don't have to explain. I'm tired, and I'm going back to bed." She got up then and walked toward the door, her hips swaying. She made no move to try to cover herself, and her body glowed in the light, either from what they shared a few moments ago or from anger, he couldn't tell. She was exposed in only the bra and panties that covered a small expanse of skin. T. J. watched her move and felt his body tighten as she came close enough he could smell her scent once again. If she were to touch him again, he wouldn't be able to control his need. Instead, she closed her door with a simple "Goodnight," leaving him on the other side of the doorway.

On the opposite side of the door, T. J.'s head rested against the cool wood, his hand resting on the door knob as if to turn it, go in and take her, to make her his. But he knew it was better this way. After this was over, she would see that her attraction to him was just a reaction to their extreme situation. She'd go off and find some exciting debonair man, and he'd be back sitting on his lake. The thought made him grit his teeth, and he turned and walked back to his room, knowing that sleep would be a very long time coming tonight.

* * * *

Sunday dawned on the lake, and the sunrise was amazing, T. J. stood watching Kelly at the window. She was watching the sun turn the water from black ink to crystal, and he had come out to do the same thing. Every ripple on the surface of the water glittered in the light, as if jewels beaded the surface. He wondered if sleep had been almost nonexistent for her, and after the night's episode, he had only dozed most of the night. He knew why. His body ached for her so deeply it scared him. Now he had made it worse by turning her away, which had hurt her.

Kelly didn't see him watching her. He knew from where he stood that her view was blocked. She wasn't ready to face him, yet T. J. could tell she would wait until she could gain some control of her emotions, until she could look him in the eye and pretend it didn't matter. That was the kind of woman she was. He watched Kelly glance at the water again. *She was probably wishing that all this was some sort of bad dream and that she would wake up in her own bed, not even knowing the name Taggert Chapel.* She turned away then from the beauty that was outside the window letting the curtains close to the light.

He stood on his deck barefooted, his pajama bottoms and a sweat shirt to keep warm in the cool morning air. Fall had settled over the lake and he looked at the leaves, the colors turned from green and lush to browns, oranges, and reds. Every time he closed his eyes, he saw her lying there, her mouth wet from his kisses, her body flushed with excitement at having his hands on her. Thoughts of having her in his bed caused his body to react. He sighed, thinking that last week he hadn't even known who Kelly Justine was, and now she was taking every spare thought in his head. She was his witness for goodness sake. She was not his type, and girls like her never fell for guys like him. He knew that. The package was pretty, but underneath he knew there was more than met the eye. He wanted to know everything about her. T. J. groaned in frustration. He was going to do the right thing even though every fiber of his being wanted to claim her. He would be honorable and stay away.

Tank padded out onto the deck and stood beside his master, staring up at him as if asking, "What's the matter with you today?"

"Come on, boy, want to go for a run by the lake?" Tank's tail thumped on the wood deck enthusiastically. T. J. smiled. A run with a best buddy could be the ticket to clearing his mind of all thoughts of Kelly and get him back on his job.

* * * *

He spotted the crime scene immediately. The familiar yellow tape, the flashing lights, curious onlookers hoping to catch a glimpse of the macabre sight, reporters hoping for a morsel to drop into their laps or for the interview of a lifetime. Police lights were flashing wildly and the press volleyed for a better view. They were all talking fast and furious into their microphones as Danny Greywood drove up. Each with a different spin on the words, but all reported the scene as it developed. Another girl had been found, this one more gruesome than the last two victims. A week had passed since the last victim had shown up by the Air Force base and Kelly had gone into hiding. Someone had tipped off the press before the police and now they were saying all the deaths were connected. Detective Greywood had been awakened by his partner, had rushed to get dressed and out of the condo amid questions from the latest girlfriend who shared his bed. He already knew this was not going to last. She had a problem with all the long hours he worked and wanted a commitment. He was not ready to give up his freedom or his job. On his way to the new crime scene, he had fielded calls from his captain, the press who had somehow gotten his name, and the mayor, who wanted this situation resolved ASAP. *Fuck! This guy is escalating, and if he isn't caught soon, a lot of shit is going to hit the proverbial fan.*

With his mouth set in a grim line, Danny pushed past the microphones and the shouted questions in his ear and went under the police tape. His partner, visibly green and looking like he might vomit his breakfast at any moment, walked up to him.

"Kirk, why is the damn press so fucking close? Do you want to lose whatever evidence we might find?" he snarled.

"Dan, the press got here first, someone called them. By the time we got here, they were snapping pictures like she was on a catwalk."

Danny thought for a moment. "Get the onlookers back to the end of the block. Corral the damn reporters who were here first. Tell them you will give a statement if you have to, then get all photos and video they got. This is an ongoing investigation, and if they don't want to give it up, arrest the fuckers on the spot. Tell them they can have it back after the family has been notified and we need to review for evidentiary purposes."

"What about freedom of press and all that bullshit?"

"Fuck that. This is some serious shit. Just tell them you'll give them a scoop later if they cooperate. That should appease them."

With a simple, "I'm on it," Kirk was gone to do his partner's bidding.

Danny walked over to the corpse covered by a white sheet, blood stains already seeping to the pristine white. *He didn't bleed this one out that's for sure,* he thought, and he nodded to Charlie, the coroner on the other two victims.

"Let me see her, Charlie." Danny hoped his voice sounded professional even though his heart thumped in his chest.

When the cover was removed from the girl's body, he was shocked at the condition of the corpse. She, too, had Kelly's name carved into her forehead.

"If the same guy did this, he sure had some anger issues," Charlie murmured. "The body is a mass of stab wounds, and her chest was left wide open, her heart half in, half out of the gaping hole."

"Shit!" The viciousness that Danny spat the word made the chubby coroner look at him with surprise. "How many stab wounds?"

"I count at least twenty-two so far, even on the genital area. There's bruising there, too. I think he raped her. I won't know for sure until I get her back on a table. He had her for a while though. I see old bruises under the new ones."

"Catalogue evidence, everything you can find on and around the body, then get her out of here so she can have a little bit of dignity."

"I did find a link between this and the other killing, though, so I do think it's your guy?"

"Apart from having our witness' name carved into her head?" Danny sighed at his sarcastic tone. "Sorry, Charlie, this is a hell of a way to wake up. What'd you find?"

"Whatever he stabbed this victim with is the same instrument he used to cut the hearts out. This may be a little more vicious, but the marks and the slicing is the same, smooth and clean."

"I'm thinking a surgical scalpel."

"Get back to me on this pronto, Charlie. This is priority, you understand?"

"You don't have to tell me twice," Charlie responded and went about his task.

Kirk jogged up to Danny as he was walking around the scene looking for anything that could tell him who this guy was. "I got everything, tapes, film. They weren't happy but they gave it up."

"Good, take it back to the station, review it all, see if anything stands out or anyone, and call me on my cell if you find anything."

"Where you off to?"

"I'm going up to look at a lake."

Detective Greywood walked over to his car and slid into the seat. He couldn't let himself think now. He had to be the professional detective and not let this bother him. He had a niece, one just a few years younger than the victims. Cop or not, he could not see this and not want to kill the man doing this. He wanted to find this guy, wrap his fingers around his neck, and squeeze slowly until he saw the life go out of him. But Daniel would let the law handle it. He made a promise he would be one of the men sitting behind that glass wall when they slipped the needle in his arm at his death sentence.

The drive to T. J.'s home was scenic, but Detective Greywood did not even notice the beauty around him. In his mind, flashes of the past few weeks kept him occupied. He went over everything repeatedly, hoping that something would jump out at him. A criminal profiler from the Charlotte branch of the FBI had contacted him during the drive. Daniel's captain had sent him the file, and he was in the process of reviewing it. He confirmed one thing Danny already knew, the guy was escalating and was hitting supernova. The guy needed to be caught and caught soon. If not, more women would die.

It was around eleven when he finally pulled into T. J.'s drive way. *T. J. heard the car on the gravel,* he thought with a small smile. He saw his friend cautiously approach the door with his revolver in hand. *He knows full well no maniac would drive up to his door.* But Danny knew how T. J. thought—it was always better to be safe that sorry. Danny saw his demeanor switch to relax mode when T. J. saw him exit the car. As he walked out onto the front deck, T. J. slipped his gun into the waist of his pants at the back.

"Come by for to check in, Danny? Thought you'd be home sleeping in on Sunday?"

"I've already been to work."

"On a Sunday? That's dedication."

"Not my call, we had another murder."

"Damn it! Come on in."

They walked in the house together. Danny looked around, remembering he had been here a long time ago. T. J. had made a lot of changes, and at another time, he would have appreciated it more.

T. J. poured coffee, and Danny asked, "Where Kelly?"

"Still upstairs in bed, I assume. What is this victim's time of death?"

"Sometime last night. Charlie is going to give me an exact time when he finishes the autopsy."

"I expect this will be like the other two."

"Not this one, T. J. He's amping up. He stabbed this one over twenty times. He cut her heart out and left it hanging out of her chest. Charlie thinks he raped her too."

"Jesus Christ!" was all T. J. could say.

"The autopsy reports came in from the other states. They're all the same, T. J., down to how the hearts are removed."

"Why didn't he take this one's heart, I wonder," T. J. mused.

"Maybe he thought it was impure or tainted," Danny replied.

"He's craving his next kill so bad it's causing him to take out his anger on theses girls. He wants Kelly."

They both whirled around at the sound of a lamp being overturned. Kelly stood in the doorway, the lamp by her feet. They stared at the woman whose face showed the horror of everything she had just heard.

Chapter Seven

"Kelly, Jesus!" T. J. started toward her, but she had already fled upstairs. He heard the door slam and he looked at Danny, who was sitting there with a sorrowful expression on his face.

"Shit, I didn't mean for her to hear like that," Danny said.

"I know, me either."

"Should I go and talk to her?"

"No, I'll do it. She hates me already, what's one more thing?"

He walked past Danny who had a raised eyebrow. "What could she possibly hate you for?"

But he was already out of the kitchen and heading upstairs. T. J. knocked on her door softly and then turned the unlocked knob, which he took as an invitation to enter. She lay on the bed facing the wall, her body racked with sobs. Hoping to soothe her, he put his hand on her shoulder and gently rubbed.

"You have to come downstairs, Kelly," he said softly.

She turned to him, tears making tracks on her cheeks. "I'm sick of being scared, of crying. For the past few weeks, it seems like it's all I've done or felt. I was just starting to feel safe."

"Then, by God, fight back! Don't let the fear fill you, fight it off, and take your life in your own hands!" he said fiercely.

"I can't fight what I can't see! Who I don't know!" she cried.

"Not the person, the fear. We'll find him, and Danny and I won't ever let anything happen to you."

"You don't even know who he is." Bitterness crept into her voice. "You can't find him!"

"We will," he said grimly. "Now I'm going downstairs to talk with Danny.

You can come down or stay here and whimper like a beaten animal."

With that, he walked out of the room and went downstairs. At Danny's questioning look, T. J. shrugged, not knowing if she was going to come down. Danny opened his mouth to speak but turned when he heard footsteps bounding down the stairs. She entered the room, wearing a blue short knit top and little shorts to match. Gone were the tears from a few moments ago, and a fierce determination showed on her face. He was, at that moment so proud of her.

"Danny, nice to see you, can I interest you in breakfast?"

"Uh, what's on the menu?"

She walked over to the fridge and looked inside. "Let's see, how does Spanish omelets, toast and sausages sound?"

"Really?" Danny said, perking up. "You can do that?

"Yes, I can."

"Well, let me tell you from a guy who has cereal every morning unless he goes to Sammy's Pancake House that sounds damn good."

"I'll get to it then," she said and turned away to prepare breakfast.

Danny watched her for a moment, then leaned over to T. J., and whispered, "She can cook right?"

T. J. grinned, patted his friend on the back, and whispering back, "Like a dream."

* * * *

Over breakfast, Danny updated them on what was going on in the investigation from his end. T. J. also let him know that in his investigation, there were only a few soldiers with blemishes on their records who had transferred to Carolina, but all had cleared. It was a dead end on his side, and both men knew it would take a next move, and it would be by the killer.

Danny sat back from his second helping of breakfast. "T. J., man, you were right. She can cook like a dream."

Both looked at the girl that sat over from them, but she wasn't listening. She was stretched to the limit. He noticed the way she pushed her food around her plate, rarely taking small bites and her withdrawn demeanor. She tried to put up a good front, making small talk and small laughs here and there. But it was there, just under the surface. Every time the conversation changed to the circumstances of her situation, her body tensed and a shadow of fear passed over her face.

"Thank you for the meal, Kelly, it was a great breakfast." Danny stood to leave.

T. J. rose with him. "I'll walk you out, Danny."

Danny paused for a moment and looked at Kelly. "I'm sorry for what you heard and how you heard it this morning."

"It's fine, detective, it isn't your fault. I can't keep pretending it isn't happening when people are dying."

"We'll get him."

"I know, Detective Greywood."

"I think you should call me Danny. After all, you made me breakfast."

She smiled at him. "Okay, Danny it is."

She rose and began to clear away remnants of breakfast and the dishes they used. Outside on the deck once again, Danny turned to T. J., "She's strung tight, T-man."

"She's handling it."

"Are you looking at the same girl I'm looking at?" Danny exclaimed. He pointed back to the direction of the kitchen. "She's tense as a bow ready to shoot an arrow."

"I can't very well do anything about it. She's in hiding, remember?"

"No one knows she's in hiding except us, and that's in Charlotte, my friend."

"There are counties outside Charlotte you know. Take her somewhere let her cut loose a bit."

"I don't thinks she cuts loose in moderation," T. J. said dryly.

"Whatever, man, just let her do it," Danny suggested as he walked to the wooden steps that led off the porch.

"I'll take your advice under advisement."

"Do that," Danny said, laughing as he walked to the car. "Maybe her cutting loose is not only just what she needs, but you as well." He drove off with a wave, and T. J. watched while he talked to the officers parked at the end of the driveway and drove off. He turned and walked back into the house and to the kitchen. Kelly had already stacked dishes in the dishwasher and was wiping down the counters as he watched her for a moment.

"You need any help?" he asked. She was startled at his voice and dropped the glass she had moved from the area she wiped.

"Sorry, sorry," she said quickly moving to clear the broken glass pieces. "Before this is over, you won't have a fragile piece of furniture or china that's not broken because of me."

He bent down to help her and they bumped heads, both coming up holding a sore spot over their eyes.

"Sorry, I'm a klutz today."

Not a klutz, just wound tight. Danny was right. She needed to forget for awhile, and cooking up a storm in his kitchen wouldn't do it.

"Why don't you go upstairs and call Abby see if she's home?"

"Oh, yeah, you're right. I don't want her to worry."

"It's afternoon now, so go chat with your friend. I'll take care of this, and then I've got some work in my office."

"Are you sure? I can clean this up before I go call."

"Nope, I insist. Go talk to your friend." He shooed her away and listened to her retreating footsteps as he continued to clean up the broken glass. He had some calls to make, but not what she thought. This had nothing to do with work.

* * * *

Abby answered on the first ring when Kelly called. "Kelly! What the hell is going on?"

Kelly opened her mouth to answer but Abby continued. "I come home, last week and you're gone and your door is padlocked and you're nowhere to be found. Then you call and tell me you're in hiding. Now I come home today and it's all over the news that another girl has been found, they're calling this guy a maniac!"

"Abby, Abby, sssshhh for a minute, I'll tell you everything." Kelly tried to soothe her long time friend trying to calm her down.

"Okay, I'm listening, but when I saw the news, I thought . . .," Abby's voice caught on a sob, and that made Kelly want to cry all over again.

The weeks that have passed had not only been hell on her but on a friendship that was closer than some sisters. Not being able to share things with her friend and visa versa was taking its toll on them both. Good or bad they were always there for each other. She didn't want Abby to worry, but she didn't want her in harm's way either.

"I'm fine, peach. Don't worry, I'm safe." She began to recount the events from Saturday morning up till now.

On the other end of the phone line, her friend listened in shocked silence.

"My God, Kelly, why didn't you call my cell? I'd have come home."

"I didn't want to ruin your weekend."

"Ruin my weekend my ass, you should have called me."

"I know, I'm sorry, but I'm safe here with Taggert."

Abby sighed. "Okay. I'm glad, so how is Taggert, and how is it staying under the same roof with that gorgeous man?"

"Complicated, we have this attraction and this heat . . . he kissed me, well, I kissed him first."

"Whoa, hold on, Kelly. You kissed him? Where? When?"

"In the guest bedroom last week, and it was like an instant connection."

"Hold your horses, this happened last week and you're telling me now?"

"It sort of slipped my mind. Then last night I had a nightmare, and he came into my room and held me."

"What did you have on?" Abby asked.

"Not much of anything." Kelly laughed. "But then we kissed and some more things. God, I wanted him then and there."

"But?"

"But he stopped. He said I wasn't his type."

Abby said angrily, "He'd be lucky if you were his type. What's his type anyway, button down school marm?"

"I don't know. I'm a little out there, Abby."

"You are not out there. You're unique, and if he's too stupid to see that, well, screw him! I might be starting to dislike this Lieutenant Chapel."

"No, Abby, he's great, and he opened his home to keep me safe. I can't force him to want me."

"I still think he's dumb," Abby muttered.

The tone in her voice made Kelly laugh. Abby's outrage for her unrequited attraction was funny, yet one of the sweetest, gestures for her friend. *Always looking out for each other to the end.* She felt tons better talking to Abby.

"Okay, peach, you, by all means, are my biggest supporter. I want you to do me a favor."

"What?"

"Go stay with Frank until this is settled, okay? He knew how to find me, which means he knows about you, and I'd just feel better if you were not there."

"Frank's been staying here with me nights."

"I know, but the two of you are safer at his place."

"Okay, I can do that. It won't be any hardship to spend some time with my handsome fireman," Abby teased.

"Yeah, I know. Maybe you should hook a wonderful, sexy, best friend up with one of his buddies," Kelly teased back.

Abby laughed. "Somehow I don't think you're going to need it."

Kelly said her goodbyes and promised to call later in the week to let her know she was okay. She had just lain down against the soft pillows of the bed and turned on the television in the room when she heard Taggert call up the stairs.

"Kelly, could you come here a second?"

She sighed, wondering what else could be going wrong now. She didn't think she could handle another death or complication in her life. She climbed off the bed, walked out the door, and looked over the banister to where he stood on the bottom step.

"What's up?"

"In all those bags that you made me lug upstairs, do you happen to have a dress and nice shoes?"

"Are you kidding me?"

He looked at her. "Yeah, I guess that's a dumb question."

"Why are you asking, Taggert?"

"Can you be ready by eight o'clock?"

"For?" Kelly inquired.

"You are a frustrating woman!" T. J. grinned as he called up the stairs. "Just be ready at eight and you'll see."

He turned and walked back into the kitchen, and then she heard the sliding door open. Tank barked excitedly, and the door close as he went outside. Kelly didn't want to admit it, but she was excited to see where they were going. She bounced into the bedroom and started pulling out different outfits she could wear. She found the perfect thing, and a grin spread across her face.

"He says I'm not his type. Well, I may not be, but it doesn't mean I can't tempt him."

She laughed out loud at the thought that ran through her head and settle back on the pillows of the bed to watch a rerun of one of her favorite shows.

* * * *

It was a little after eight, and Taggert paced downstairs muttering to himself. "I told her to be ready by eight, how hard is it to be punctual?"

"Kelly!" he yelled up the stairs for the fifth time.

"Okay, I'm coming, jeez," Kelly yelled back while closing her bedroom door. "When you say eight, you should technically say seven-thirty that way I have some leeway."

"Well, excuse me. I didn't know I had to set my clock to Kelly-time and what took—"

Kelly could practically see the words die in Taggert's throat when he saw her come down the stairs. Kelly was wearing a knee-length, wine red halter dress that had a slit up each side exposing her smooth, creamy thighs. She had decided to wear her hair down in silky waves that framed her face, and on her feet were sandals with stiletto heels the same color of the dress that were tied around her ankles in a fashionable bow.

"What do you think?" she asked Taggert and did a little twirl. The twirl was for him to see her little surprise. The dress had no back down to her waist, which he noticed.

He swallowed as if his mouth was dry before answering. "Uh, fine, you look fine, yeah we should go."

"Okay, I'm ready." She hid a smile as she walked to the door.

She had gotten the response she had wanted, and she happily walked out onto the veranda and waited until he locked the door. The drive was quiet. Neither of them said much, but when she looked over at him and he glanced away from the road for a second their gazes connected. She smiled and her eyes sparkled.

Taggert took her to a wonderfully authentic Italian restaurant farther up the lake front, and from the time they walked in, the scents off wines sauces and pasta assaulted her senses. Kelly looked around and smiled in delight that there was a dance floor where some couples were swaying in each other arms to a soft melody. They were seated by the hostess at one of the tables outside on the balcony. There were string lights hanging from the rafters and threaded through the branches of small trees. The night was cool but still warm enough to eat outside.

"Well, what do you think?" Taggert asked.

"It's very nice, but why did you decide to do this?"

"I am trying to pay you back for all those meals."

"Pay back, hmmmm?"

He nodded. "Yup. You have been feeding me from day one when I came to your apartment that Friday night, remember?"

"It slipped my mind. A lot has happened since that Friday."

Taggert placed his hand over hers on the table. "Tonight is for you not to think about that."

A waiter walked up to their table to take their drink order. T. J. ordered a Michelob Dark and Kelly ordered a vodka cranberry.

Taggert's eyebrows rose when she asked with a smile, "You thought I'd be ordering a wine spritzer?"

He held up his hand in surrender. "Hey, I never said that. I've learned never to assume with you."

"You shouldn't. If you think you can ever figure me out then I've become boring."

"Sometimes boring is good."

"It works on some people, on me no."

"Why is that, Kelly Justine? What makes you want to be unlike everyone else?"

"Because I am, I like to think I am a fabulous freak of nature." She laughed.

"That doesn't answer my question."

"Well, then let me answer your question." But just as she was about to, the waiter came back with their drinks, placed them on the table, and took their dinner orders. Kelly took a sip and nodded in approval of the drink. She definitely needed a stiff belt after the time she'd been having lately.

"You never answered my question," Taggert remarked.

Her mind had wandered off. "What? Oh, okay, to be like everyone else means that somewhere along the line I lost my identity, and then who am I?"

With that, she went back to sipping her drink. She felt Taggert watching her and wondered if he was thinking that there was more to her than met the eye, more thoughts and fears that she never shared but was willing to. The problem was, would he want to dare find out what else there was to her?

* * * *

They had found his message, and they were afraid, he thought with glee. He was the unknown figure that haunted their dreams, Kelly's dreams. He could almost rub his hands together in happiness, knowing he was one step ahead of them. There was no way to trace the bodies. He'd made sure that would never be a possibility; and now he stood outside the door of the man who thought he was keeping Kelly safe. Safe from him! He scoffed at the idea. He was her salvation, and she had nothing to fear from him. She was his dove after all, handpicked to mark his transformation into an immortal. But the lieutenant would have to die, he was certain of that. He came to that conclusion as the hearts beat around him, praising him. The lieutenant would stand in his way, and that could not be allowed.

The sliding door opened easily, and he stood there in the dim stillness of the kitchen. He heard the low growl of the big stupid animal that protected the house, knowing it wasn't even an issue. He had forethought and from the pocket of his coat brought out a succulent steak with a little something extra. He watched the dumb dog gobble up the meat and then petted and rubbed him until he fell asleep.

It was a nice house. He liked the look, and he liked the lieutenant's tastes. They could have been friends, if he were not beyond having mortal friends. But, nonetheless, it was a nice house. He went up the stairs and found the room Kelly was using. In the drawers were lacy panties and bras. Her clothes were skimpy, almost nothing, and he couldn't have his dove wearing whore clothes. The gleam of sharp stainless steel scissors caught the low light as he withdrew them from his pocket. The first snip was like a kid having a treat of candy. Soon he was cutting and shredding her clothes, leaving only the things he thought were suitable. He left the sexy underwear because a lady should always have pretty things under her clothing and took a few things for him.

On his way downstairs, he made sure he left another message for them to find. This one would be loud and clear. There was also a tiny little friend hidden so he would have ears in the house. He went out the way he came and stopped once again to pet the dog, which was actually snoring in his sleep. He liked dogs, had even wanted one as a child. When he had found one and brought it home, his mother told him to take it away. When he refused, she did it for him, in the unkindest of ways, by drowning it in a mop bucket while he watched with tears on his cheeks. She had sat him down after the dog was gone and had let him know that he was meant for more than being a keeper of a lower species. It was then she let him know he was chosen and his path in life. From then on, he knew that he could love nothing or no one because all were meant to serve him in one way or another. His mother's heart had been the first taken, and it had been with him ever since. Her heart sat in a position of authority, for she was the one that showed him the purpose for his existence. He slid the door close once again and walked back through the woods where he came. The police who were on duty had gone to dinner when the lieutenant took his dove out. He remembered how she was dressed, like some sort of slut from the streets. The lowly lieutenant would be punished for that. They would know he had been there soon enough, that there was nowhere to hide from him.

Chapter Eight

Home again, Kelly thought. It had been a wonderful evening. They had talked and laughed over a dinner of penne pasta and seafood with a cream sauce. She'd found out that Taggert was thirty-eight, and he was an only child to a single mom who was an artist. He opened up about himself to her, explaining that he had joined the military to straighten his life out and then had found out that he liked the life of an army man. During dinner, Kelly found herself thinking less about being stalked by a killer and more about being with Taggert. She could see herself with him. The only snag was that his interest in her was only as her protector. There was a sexual energy between them, that was a definite fact, but beyond that, she could not be sure, and sex could never be the only thing.

Taggart pulled the truck into its usual spot while Kelly was trying to convince him to listen to some of her CDs. He stayed firm, saying the newer music genres were okay but the classics could never be beat.

"I never said Pink Floyd wasn't good, Taggert," she said as she closed the truck door. "I have a few of their CDs. But you could mix some Audioslave and maybe some reggae in every now and again to spice it up."

"Uh, I like my music to relax me and not make me hyper one moment to the next."

"Hey, now, I have music to suit my every mood, and I listen to it accordingly. Taggert, doesn't Tank usually come running out here by now?" she asked. She had become accustomed to him running out and barking when they came back home. Now there was absolute silence, not even a bark from the house.

Taggert looked around. "Hmm, maybe he got stuck in the mud room again."

"Why would that dog keep going into the room when he knows it's too small for him?" Kelly said as they walked up the steps.

"His brain is a marshmallow."

They both laughed. As they stepped through the front door, the laughter died on their lips. There on the wall at the top of the stairs written in black letters on the wall, "FOUND YOU!"

T. J. pulled her back onto the verandah pulling out his cell phone as he moved. Kelly was too scared, too shocked to even utter a sound. *He's found me! Even out here, he found me!* She wrapped her arms around herself and tried to control her body that had begun to shake. She barely heard Taggert on the phone.

"Danny, get your people out here now!" he barked. "The motherfucker's been in my goddamn house!"

He slammed the cell phone closed and looked around at Kelly, who was standing in the corner next to the rail. The cops had come running up the driveway when they saw them come out of the house. With guns pulled, the two men came up the steps.

"Search the house thoroughly. I'll start downstairs," he ordered. "Kelly, you stay out here until I give you the okay."

She nodded stiffly, not moving from where she stood. Taggert looked at her for a moment and then hurried inside. Moments later, he came out and found her still there in the corner by the rail. Kelly felt so fragile she felt like she was trying to hide herself in a tiny space where the wall and the rails met. She hadn't even noticed when he came back outside. When Taggert touched her shoulder, she jumped like a cat when someone stepped on its tail.

"The house is clear, you can come in now."

"I'd prefer to stay out here for now," she said softly

He tried his hardest to get her inside. The wind had picked up, coming off the lake, and the night was cold, but Kelly barely felt it. She was numb from the inside out.

"Kelly, it's cold out here, and I need you anyway. Tank's in the kitchen. He's been drugged. I need you to sit with him until he wakes up."

"How do you know he was drugged?"

"He's all groggy and bleary eyed. He threw up on the floor, some undigested meat and half of a sleeping pill."

"That's how he got it into Tank's system."

"Poor Tank. Shouldn't he go to the vet?"

"He'll be fine. We'll watch him for a bit and see if he perks up. That's why I need you in there with him."

"Poor baby." Her concern for the dog she had first mirrored to Cujo was immediate. He was loveable, and when she was cooking, she fed him bits and pieces so they had become fast friends. Kelly hurried inside in front of Taggert, headed straight to the kitchen, and sat on the floor beside the dog that had begun to whine in a pitiful way as he woke up. She knew what Taggart was trying to do. Taking care of the dog would keep her mind on something else for a few minutes.

* * * *

T. J. watched her pet and croon to the dog, then left the room silently to continue to look around and to wait for Danny to show up. He went to his office to see if anything had been moved or taken. Surprisingly enough, his office was the exact way he had left it. This guy didn't even seem to want to know if T. J. had found out who he was or what he knew. T. J. saw the flashing lights from through the trees that lined the street before the turn to his driveway. He looked at his watch—half an hour had already passed since they came home. By the time he walked out the front door, the tires of Danny car and two other police cars were screeching to a halt in his driveway.

"We hauled ass up here, T-man." Danny said. "What do we have?"

"What we have is the sick fucker broke into my house, drugged my dog, and cut up all of Kelly's clothes."

Danny turned and started to bark orders at the four officers in uniform that came with him. "You two start processing from where he entered, and you two check the back and the woods surrounding it, see if you get anything."

Danny turned to T. J. "Where's Kelly?"

"She's inside sitting with the dog. Danny, we have to figure out a way to keep her safe because this guy is getting his info somewhere and even if we move her again, he's going to find her."

"I know but I'm out of options except putting her in a safe house."

"I might have an idea but it would mean us working under the radar." T. J.'s mind was working on an idea just as a plan B. It seemed he would need it sooner rather than later.

"Okay, tell me what you got."

"Not now, let's get this done and these guys out of here."

"I can tell you something, Danny, the man is one cocky son of a bitch, and he isn't going to stop until we stop him."

"And we will," Danny replied.

In the kitchen, Kelly was nowhere to be found. Danny and T. J. went up the stairs together and found her in the room that she slept in sitting on the floor in the midst of all her shredded and ripped clothing. She looked up as they walked in with tears streaming down her face.

"Why . . . why would he do this?" she asked, gesturing around to the bits of fabric across the floor.

Danny crouched down to the floor and held her hand. "I don't know, but clothes are nothing. I promise he won't get you."

"I can't do this anymore. I can't feel like this anymore! I'm scared all the time, and I'm not safe anywhere!" she cried.

"You're safe with us, Kelly," T. J. said. "I have a plan, but I don't want to talk about it here."

"Get together whatever's left of your things. We're going to be staying at a hotel for a few nights."

"Danny, finish up here then meet us at this address." He scribbled on a piece of note paper and handed it to the detective. "The three of us are going to sit, and I'll tell you my plan."

While Kelly piled her toiletries and some of her clothes that weren't destroyed into a bag, Danny read something else that T. J. had written on the paper and then gave him a questioning look.

"What's you're plan, T-man?" Danny asked curiously.

"Just do that and get back to the address right after. I've got to talk to my superior for approval, but this way, we can be sure if he comes looking we'll know exactly who he is." T. J.'s tone was grim. Anger for what this bastard was doing to Kelly made him want to hit something.

"Okay, I'll see you there," Danny said and as he walked out of the room, he looked over at Kelly and said to her "Look at it this way, babe, you get to go on a wild shopping spree to replace this stuff." That comment earned Danny a smile, and he went downstairs to get things done.

T. J. left Kelly to finish packing her things, went to his room, and packed some of his civilian clothes in a duffel bag. He came back to her room ten minutes later.

"Ready?"

"I guess so."

"We have to take a little side trip to drop off Tank."

"Where are we taking him?"

"To my mom's place."

They came down the stairs together. "Lock up when you're done, Danny."

His friend raised his hand to let him know he would. T. J. loaded a still groggy but moving Tank into the back of the truck and then he and Kelly were off down the driveway.

* * * *

Maria Chapel lived in Shelby, North Carolina, in an old-fashioned farmhouse. As they drove up, the patio light came on and a tall willowy woman stepped out onto the wooden floor. Maria waved when she saw her son step out of the truck. When a young woman got out of the passenger side, Maria looked curiously at her son.

"T. J., honey, what are you doing here?" she asked. "And who is this tiny creature you brought with you?"

"Mom, you're not that big yourself." T. J. laughed and embraced the woman who had raised him tough even though she was a single parent.

"I'm bigger than her. How tall are you honey?"

Kelly answered, "I'm five-three, ma'am."

"Listen to that accent! Well, you're no bigger than a pixie."

She continued on as they walked in the house. "I like to paint fairies and fairytale folk. I like the mystical in life, and we all should believe in a little magic, shouldn't we?"

The young woman nodded as Maria talked. She seated them down at the kitchen table and began to make coffee.

"Kelly likes fairies as well. She has lots of prints in her home, Mom," T. J. cut in.

"Oh, that's wonderful. A fellow whimsical woman. Kelly, is it? How do you like your coffee?"

"Yes, ma'am, we should always believe in a little magic," Kelly replied. "I'm trying to quit coffee, no thank you."

"Oh pish-posh. One cup isn't going to do anything but give you a little zing."

T. J. shook his head at Kelly to let her know it was no use arguing with his mother. She would just do as she pleased anyway.

"Cream, no sugar, please," Kelly said.

"Good, too much sugar isn't good for you." Maria smiled broadly at the two sitting at her kitchen table. "So what do you do for a living, Kelly?"

"I'm a companion to two elderly ladies. I give them physical therapy and keep them out of trouble."

"Why keep them out of trouble, dear?"

Kelly's laugh rang out in the kitchen. "They're a bit feisty."

Maria joined in with Kelly. She liked the girl almost immediately. She seemed bubbly and upbeat, but she could tell something was wrong. Her eyes looked tired, and her hands shook a little.

"Kelly, do you believe in auras?" Maria asked. "You have a lovely aura, shimmering reds and oranges. I think that you could be—"

"Mom," T. J. cut in again before his mother could start another conversation about crystals and meditation. "I need you to take care of Tank for a bit until I come and get him."

"Okay, but I could have driven out to your place and fed him."

"Mom, it's a little more complicated than that. Kelly is being stalked by the killer on the news. She was staying at my place, and he broke in. We're going to have to go incognito for a while."

Maria listened as T. J. filled her in on what had been going on and about the break in at his house. At the end of his story, she patted Kelly's hand with concern etched on her face.

"You poor girl," she said to Kelly and then to T. J. "And here I was thinking you finally brought a girl home to meet me. Of course, you can stay here."

"Mom, no," T. J. interjected. "We can't stay here. He found my place, he'll find yours, and I don't want you in that kind of danger. We're going much farther."

"T. J., I think she'd be safe—" Maria started.

"Mom, no!"

"Taggert Julius Chapel, you do *not* take that tone with me!" Maria cut through sharply.

"Sorry, Mom."

Maria took in Kelly's face as she listened to the exchange between mother and son with a huge grin on her face. She looked at her son, who looked like a scolded schoolboy, and Kelly was enjoying every moment of it.

"Stop laughing at me," T. J. hissed between gritted teeth to Kelly.

"Why should I, Taggert Julius? You should never use that tone with your mom," Kelly teased.

"I was not using a tone."

Kelly poked him. "Yes you were."

Maria Chapel watched the exchange between her son and the lovely woman sitting at her table with a secret smile. There was more there than they were letting on. "All right, I can understand your not staying here, but you promise to be safe honey and keep her safe too."

"I will, Mom."

T. J. hugged his mother tight when they got up to leave, and then she in turn hugged Kelly. Maria was delighted with the open affection that Kelly showed her. She could feel Kelly's tension, but as a mother, she could see the underlying emotions the woman was forming for her son. She sent up a protection prayer to the Goddess and hoped to continue the conversation with Kelly about auras and the mystical when her trouble was over. She couldn't even imagine her fear of coming to a place where she was supposed to be safe and seeing the words "Found you" on the wall. It was going to take a while for the poor girl to ever be able to feel safe again.

"Before you go, Kelly, here I want you to have this. It will keep you safe." Maria went over to a chest she kept on her writing desk and pulled out a necklace made of blue beads and amber crystals. In the center of the necklace was a large amber stone in the shape of an oval.

"It's lovely, Ms. Chapel, but I can't accept it." Kelly shook her head, hesitating to take the gift.

Maria admonished her. "Nonsense. It's a gift, a few rocks and beads. I make them all the time. I want you to have it, and it's Maria."

Kelly looked at T. J. who nodded his head for her to take it. Maria saw the silent exchange and smiled to herself. This was a good thing for her son.

"Well, thank you so much, Ms. Cha—Maria."

"It's my pleasure, Kelly," Maria replied, hugging Kelly once again.

"Now go, T. J., and bring her back to see me when this is over."

"I will, Momv," T. J. said and kissed his mother's cheek once again.

Maria watched the truck drive off with her son and his companion inside. She was worried, but she knew her son could take care of himself. She petted Tank's head who sat beside her on the porch. "Don't worry, Tanky, baby. He'll be back soon, and I don't think he'll be alone." She had the sneaky suspicion that she would be seeing Kelly a lot more when this was over. After all, a mother's instinct is never wrong.

* * * *

Kelly wondered what T. J.'s plan was. After they left his mother, he took the route to uptown and drove right to the Marriott Hotel. She didn't know when he did it, but he had booked three rooms. She asked why three rooms, but before he could respond, Danny strolled into the hotel lobby with a suitcase. He was not dressed in his usual suit and tie, but in casual slacks and a T-shirt. He looked completely different and less intimidating.

Kelly gave him a huge smile as he came up to them, and with a sexy drawl, she said, "Why, detective, I like the new look."

He grinned at her. "Glad you approve."

"If you two are done adoring Danny's look, we should go and talk," Taggert said.

On the fifth floor, the three rooms Taggert booked were all in a row with Kelly's in the middle and doors within joined them. He had picked these rooms specifically because if something happened, he and Danny could get to her immediately.

"Five minutes to put your stuff away. Then we all meet in Kelly's room. I'll explain everything then," Taggert said before going to his room and closing the door.

Danny looked at Kelly and winked which earned him another brilliant smile. "Well, hop to it, Ms. Kelly. Don't want to keep the lieutenant waiting."

With a mock salute, Kelly went into her room and closed the door. She looked around the room, which had a small kitchen area, and frowned. She assumed they would be eating a lot of fast food and made a note to ask for salads if and when they went to eat. The door that separated her and Taggert's room opened, and he strode in.

Kelly stared at him with an irritated glare. "Well, you could have knocked."

"You knew I was coming."

"Still that was just rude. What if I had been naked or something?"

With a raised eyebrow he looked at her as if picturing her naked. Then a knock came from Danny's side of the door just before she could see where this could lead. *Damn!*

"Come on in," she called. "See, he was polite enough to knock."

"What'd I miss?" Danny asked.

"Taggert is rude."

"I am not rude."

"Well, he knocked, you didn't. That means rude."

Danny listened to the words volley back and forth. "Do you two need some alone time 'cause I can go back to my room and watch HBO."

"Could we please just get on with this? It is after midnight, and I want to get some sleep sometime!" Taggert's irritation was evident in his voice.

"Fine, still rude, though," Kelly said, needing to get the last word in.

Taggert shot her a dark look, and she sat back and folded her lips in making a locking motion with her fingers on her lips. Danny was grinning at the comical expression on her face and that caused T. J. to give him the same dark look.

"Okay, here's the situation. We know this guy is openly stalking Kelly, and he has no intention of stopping. We don't know who he is, but he obviously has either a connection in the police force or enough pull to get info, maybe both."

"So what do you have planned, T. J.?" Danny asked.

"We're going to take him out of his element, and keep her safe as well."

"How are we going to do that?" Kelly piped in.

"We are taking you home," T. J. said simply.

"Back to my apartment?" she asked sharply. "He got in there, he found me there."

"Yeah, T-man, that's not a good place—"

"No, no, not the apartment. We're taking her to Barbados."

* * * *

"What? What!" Kelly stammered.

"Hear me out," T. J. said even before Danny could open his mouth.

"Here's how I look at it. He knows somehow where we put her, and like I said, this guy has a connection somewhere, who's feeding him info and keeping him hidden. We're basically trying to protect her from a ghost here, but we take her to Barbados, and we'll have the upper hand. He'll have to fly out, and there'll be a trail, possibly even a name. I'll have someone I can trust on it from this end, and down there we can control the situation better. Whoever it is will stand out like a sore thumb."

"I see where you're coming from, so that's why my lieutenant had my vacation papers ready when I went into the precinct." Danny sat back in his chair.

"That's right. The cover here is that the murders got to you, and you were given leave. You're off the case. My superiors have already given me the go ahead, anything to get this guy out of the papers here."

Kelly, who had been listening intently to the conversation, then asked, "What about my family there, Taggert? Won't this put them in danger?"

"I don't think so. You have brothers on the island and family. If necessary many different hiding places, and he can't know them all because I myself don't know them all."

"So you did a background check on me and my family."

"Yes. I went more in-depth into your background, because this idea was in the back of my head as a plan B."

"I have to admit the thought of going back home is exciting. I haven't been there for a bit. I would feel ten times safer around my family. So I guess I'm going home."

Danny rubbed his face and with a grin stated, "I've always wanted to see the islands, the sun the sea, the exotic women, while protecting you, of course, Kelly."

Kelly leaned over and playfully punched him in the shoulder, then turned to T. J. "So when do we leave?"

"We leave in two days. Until then, Kelly, you are not to leave this room, understood?" T. J. said.

"And don't tell Abby where you are until we are on the island."

"Why Abby would never tell—"

"I know she wouldn't, but we want her safe, without any knowledge, just in case."

"Understood perfectly, lieutenant," she replied somberly.

So that's it. She's going home to Barbados, and hopefully when she returns, she will have her life back, T. J. thought. "Now since we are all updated and clear, I suggest we get some sleep."

Danny strolled to the door to his room and, with a casual wave behind him, said, "Night all."

"Goodnight," they responded in unison.

"Well, I'm going to go to my room."

"Okay. Your mom is nice, by the way. I like her."

"She liked you too Kelly." T. J. hesitated at the door to his room "You know you're going to come out on top of this."

"I trust you to keep me safe, Taggert, I really do."

He looked at her, and there was complete trust in her eyes. He felt strong all of a sudden, like her trust could make him conquer the world. He closed the door to his room and moved around quietly getting ready to go to bed. He was used to sleeping in different places so his routine never changed. After spending eighteen months in Iraq sleeping on a cot in a makeshift trailer with only a few personal possessions, and years before that, he had been all over the world, wherever his assignment at the time took him. He was just glad most of the time that there was a bed when he traveled. Staying at the Marriott was not a hardship in the least.

Lying in bed with his eyes closed, thinking about Kelly, he knew he was accustomed to moving around, but he also knew that she just wanted to be back at home in her own space. He saw the easy exchange between Danny and her and wished somehow it were like that with them instead. To be casual meant friends, but that was the problem. She wanted to be more than friends, and the unknown made him feel out of his element. With work, he was always in control. A relationship with Kelly would spiral into something he could not chart. It didn't mean that he couldn't almost taste her on his lips when he thought about her. In the midst of his thoughts, he felt the covers on his bed slide back, and a soft, warm body curve next to him.

"Let me sleep here tonight, Taggert," she whispered. "Just hold me until I fall asleep."

T. J. couldn't tell her no, but he had to admit to himself, having her in his arms was good. She needed it and so did he. He wanted this to be the only place she would feel safe, next to him with his arms holding her close, fighting away the fear and the bad dreams.

He said nothing as she snuggled close to him. His body surged to life from having her pressed against his side. He knew what she needed right then was security. He turned to her and pulled her into his arms so her back was against his chest and the rest of her body pressed intimately against him. T. J. pressed his face against her neck and inhaled the smell of her hair. He let himself feel just for a little bit. His chest filled with something new, a sensation that was unlike anything he'd felt for any other woman in his life. Safe in T. J.'s strong arms, Kelly fell asleep and soon T. J. did as well.

* * * *

Kelly slowly opened her eyes to find T. J.'s face right next to hers. In the middle of the night, they had turned to each other. She studied his face relaxed in sleep. His beard had grown in a little, and his lips were slightly parted. A little snore came from him, and she smiled. She could wake up every morning and do this, watch him while he slept. Her eyes widened in shock, she knew then that she felt more than just lust for Taggert, that somewhere in the chaos of the last few weeks she fallen for the guy who was her protector. The same guy who let her know that he wasn't interested in her in that way. She closed her eyes and held back a moan of despair. How could she have been so stupid to fall for a man who couldn't or wouldn't return her feelings?

Kelly opened her eyes once again to look at T. J. This time she was met by his gray gaze. They stared at each other, neither saying a word until T. J. took her lips in a kiss. The stubble on his face created a wonderful friction as he kissed her. His tongue slid deep into her mouth, drinking her in, and she gave willingly. Her hand slipped around his neck and pulled him closer. He pulled her to him so she was lying across his chest.

"Hey, where's the other two of this threesome?" Danny called out as he opened the door to T. J. room. "Ah shit . . . um, sorry, guys. I didn't know you were busy, I'll just go back to my room, ah yeah, my room." Danny was stumbling over his words, and he stepped back into Kelly's room. Kelly had her face buried in T. J.'s neck, and she shook with laughter. T. J. was even smiling watching the big man stumble around his words.

"I think that's our cue to get up, Taggert."

"I guess so. I do have some arrangements to make for our trip."

"Our trip," Kelly echoed. "For a minute, I almost forgot about that."

"Maybe I'll make you forget about it again soon," Taggert said and rolled out of bed.

Kelly watched him stroll into the bathroom, whistling under his breath. *What the hell does he mean by that?* She shrugged and got up to go to her room. The kiss was still on her mind and T. J.'s reactions confused her, hot and cold like the faucets on a sink. Men called women confusing. They were so unreadable. Sometimes, men needed to come with instruction manuals. In her room, she pulled out clothes to wear after her shower, making a promise to herself to replace every stitch that the killer destroyed. He may have shredded her material possessions, but she swore he would not destroy her. She wouldn't let him.

Chapter Nine

Danny heard a knock on his door. Knowing no killer–stalker would knock on the door, he walked over to it with his gun in hand because his training had taught him to be cautious in situations like this. He visibly relaxed after looking through the peephole and seeing T. J. standing on the other side of the door.

"Hey, man, sorry about before. I didn't know you and Kelly were . . . well, you know," Danny said blushing as he talked.

"We weren't doing anything, Dan."

"Looked like something to me, and who could blame you. She is a fine-looking chick."

"It was just a kiss. She slept in my bed. She felt safer there, and it just happened. And why am I explaining to you anyway?" T. J. said with frustration. He wished he could understand what was going on himself and trying to explain it to someone else was just as bad.

Danny held up his hands in defense. "I don't know, T-man, you just are. Maybe you feel like you have to. Let me ask you question, is this a first kiss or has it happened before?"

Danny took T. J.'s nonresponse as an affirmative to the question and continued. "T-man, far be it for me to say, but Kelly is in a fragile place, and things could get complicated."

"Don't you think I know that?" T. J. snapped.

"All I'm saying is she doesn't seem to be the type that just fools around for kicks. Remember that, okay, buddy?"

"I'm going to go get things arranged for our trip. Keep an eye on her," was T. J.'s only response.

T. J. strode out the door, and Danny went over to the phone and ordered breakfast for two. He decided to play devil's advocate to see just how far T. J. was into Kelly. It would be very interesting to watch it play out.

Danny knocked on Kelly's door, and when she opened it, he pushed a cart in with the smell of steaming coffee coming from a pot.

"Is this some kind of conspiracy?" Kelly asked with resignation.

"Is what a conspiracy?" Danny asked.

"I'm trying to quit coffee, but since this mess started, someone is always tempting me with it."

"Oh, yeah, you did say that the first night after you saw . . . well, after what you saw. I could call down and get you some juice."

"No, it's okay. I smelled it. I've got to have it now."

Danny read the front of her T-shirt. "Smack your ass, huh?"

"I practice what I preach," she teased. "One of the few things the idiot didn't destroy. I guess he missed this one."

"I could oblige if you want," he said jokingly

Kelly laughed as she opened one of the covers to find a steaming omelet. "No thank you. You keep those big paws off my tush."

"Aw, man, no fair."

The banter continued throughout the omelets and the three cups of coffee Kelly drank. She convinced Danny that the Monday morning blues could be erased by Monday morning cartoons. As they sat on the floor, he watched her laugh uproariously at some silly antic by an animated character. He felt a brotherly bond to her, like he should protect her like a big brother would his baby sister. By noon, T. J. wasn't back, and Danny could see Kelly was already going stir-crazy in the hotel room. She was a girl accustomed to going and doing as she pleased, and the outdoors were her heaven especially in the fall. She watched cartoons with Danny, even played cards, but that only kept her interest for a short time. Two days inside would make her stir crazy.

"What time is it now, Daniel?"

"When did the whole calling me Daniel thing start?"

"When I saw you flinch the first few times I said it."

"It's irritating the hell out of me."

"I know, but I'm bored, Daniel." she smiled when she saw him flinch once again.

"You know you're like a big kid, watching cartoons, teasing me."

"It keeps me young at heart. You should try it sometime."

"I'll get right on that when I retire."

"Come on, be spontaneous." She gave him a slanted look that made Danny gulp. "Daniel," she said with a sexy purring voice. "I'm bored. Let's do it. You know you want to."

Danny heard the purr in her voice and backed up. "Now, wait a minute, Kelly. You're not that bored."

"Yes, I am, and I want to do it," she said, walking slowly toward him as he kept backing up. Danny looked round for an escape route but found none.

"Let's do it Daniel," she repeated. "Let's order a pay-per-view movie and get popcorn."

"Wait, I don't want to sleep—say what?"

At his confused, then relieved, expression, Kelly threw herself on the bed laughing. With tears in her eyes, she asked, "What did you think I meant, you nut?"

"That's was a dirty trick."

"It wasn't. You just jumped to conclusions."

"Yeah, well, the voice and the I'm-a-sexy-kitty walk, I was supposed to think movie?"

"Sexy kitty?" Kelly was howling with laughter once again. "Who have you been dating?"

"Do you want to get the movie or what?"

"Yes, Daniel," she said, trying to keep a straight face. "I pick and you get microwaveable popcorn from room service."

"Anything to get off this conversation," he muttered under his breath and went to the phone. Still grinning from ear to ear, Kelly walked over and picked up the remote to see what the hotel was offering.

Danny looked up as T. J. walked in a little later on. Both were on the floor and watching the television intently. Kelly's head rested in Danny's lap, and her hand buried in a bag of popcorn. The music became suspenseful, and Kelly covered her face with her fingers but still peeked through them. Danny looked away from T. J. and back to the TV, and he leaned forward in anticipation of the impending doom of the characters in the movie grabbing a handful of popcorn from the bag that Kelly held. He secretly smiled, knowing the cozy picture that they made on the floor made T. J. grit his teeth.

"Aren't we having fun?" T. J. asked sarcastically.

Kelly threw a handful of popcorn at him. "Ssssh, Taggert, they're going to find the zombies now."

"Oh, well, pardon me for interrupting. I'll just leave you to it then, since you don't have anything else to worry about other than zombies. Isn't there someone after you?"

"Low blow, Taggert. Danny, turn it off please. It's obvious he has something to say," Kelly said quietly.

She moved off the floor to a sitting position on the bed and Danny turned off the TV. Danny gave T. J. a hard look. "That was a dumbass thing to say."

There was a look of shame on T. J.'s face, but he masked it quickly before speaking in a brisk, military-like tone. "All right, I took a bit longer than I expected, but I have everything set up. Three tickets to leave for Barbados tomorrow night."

"What time is the flight?" Kelly asked. "Do we go through JFK in New York or Miami?"

"It's at ten p.m., and New York is closer and quicker."

"So that means we should arrive in Barbados around three or four a.m. barring delays?"

Danny piped in, "What about the other aspects of our little trip?"

"It's all in place. I have a Sergeant in charge of it on this end. He's going to monitor any flights out of Charlotte for our destination, especially any with military discounts or titles. He'll get the flight manifest and send them directly to me, and from there, we should be able to narrow the search down. It's the end of September now, and from what I hear, there's a lull in tourism, especially in the Caribbean."

"Meaning what, exactly?" Kelly asked.

"Meaning there aren't many flights out of Charlotte to Barbados, and he'll be easy to track," Danny supplied. He knew exactly where T. J. was going wit this plan, and it was ingenious.

"Uh, one little question. He's been smart enough to keep the cops and you off his trail. Don't you think he'll figure it out?"

"Kelly, that's not the point. If he figures it out, I'm assuming that he's so obsessed with you, he'll still follow you."

"Or he'll think we're so stupid for thinking that we could hide you from him that he'll come to prove us wrong. Either way, we have him," Danny added.

"And I'm the bait?"

"We'll be right there, bait," Danny said and fondly patted her on the head. She smiled at him and punched him in the arm, a gesture that caused him to grin. Kelly was a trip to be around, even in this hard time.

With a sweet smile, T. J. said, "You'll be able to forget your troubles on the beach."

"You reminded me a few minutes ago that I should keep my mind on my troubles. Someone after me, remember?" Kelly replied in a surly voice. "No need to try to butter me up. This is a mission, and I know that."

"Ouch," Danny said under his breath and hid a smile. *Oh, you stepped into it now, buddy.*

"I'm tired. Could you two go talk somewhere else?"

They walked toward Danny's door and looked at her before going into his room. Behind them they heard the door click.

"Good going, T. J. Why'd you have to go and bring her down?" Danny smacked T. J. upside the head lightly.

"I didn't do anything. I just saw her with her head in your lap, and it irked me a little. That stuff just slipped out. And keep your big mitts off me."

"Uh-huh, so you were jealous?"

"No," he said hastily. "I just . . . well, it bothered me, okay!"

"The man doth protest too much."

"I'm not protesting, I thought it was inappropriate."

"Why was it inappropriate?" Danny drawled. He sat back and watched T. J. pace the room.

"Will you forget it, Danny?"

"Okay, then I guess when we are on the tropical island I can dance to the conga with Kelly. She probably looks great in a bikini with that—"

At T. J.'s low growl Danny laughed, his assumption about T. J.'s feelings for Kelly was right on the ball. "Face it, lieutenant, you got it bad for the little Caribbean momma in the next room." He laced his fingers behind his head and looked at T. J. squarely. "So either you do something about it or watch other men drool over her when she walks down the beach."

"I'm supposed to protect her, Danny. It's against the rules."

"Fuck the rules, she's not a soldier. She's a woman, a woman who's afraid and getting mixed signals from you. Figure it out, and quick, because she has goddamn feelings for you. Be with her or let her alone!"

"Since when did you become her defender?"

"Since now. She makes me feel like a big bother, man, and I ain't going to see her hurt, so think on that." Danny held up one big hand and folded it into a fist. "Or this will be the mitt you'll be feeling next, T-man."

"Remember who taught you all those combat moves." T. J. grinned.

"Yeah, but I'm still bigger than you, and a brawler." They had a mutual understanding and their friendship was important. Teasing about a fight was something they did from the old days back in the service together.

"We'll get dinner uptown later, so I'm going to get showered and chill a while."

"Knock when you're ready to leave," Danny said.

* * * *

T. J. went through the door to the hallway and went to his room. He didn't want to disturb her, and he didn't think he could face her yet after how he had reacted. She had wanted to forget for just a little bit, and he had acted like an idiot. He looked at the door that separated his room from Kelly's. When he tried the doorknob, he discovered she'd locked him out as well. He ran his hand through his hair in frustration and flopped down on his back on the bed.

His life had been so simple, and then Kelly just blew in like one of the hurricanes that whirled in the ocean before destroying an island. Now he didn't know which end was up where his emotions were concerned. He knew he couldn't get her out of his mind, out of his dreams. He had woken up with a hard-on almost every night even when he hardly knew her. The shimmer of her skin was like candlelight flickered against it. Her lips were so soft and full, he wanted to bite them every time he kissed her, and in his dreams, he did. He felt his body even react to the thoughts that swirled around in his head. This was getting him nowhere, so he got up and went into the shower in hopes that under the spray of the hot water, he could get his thoughts in check. Somewhere in the back of his mind, he heard his mom say, *"You think too much."* That could be a possibility. Maybe he should shut his mind off and just feel for a change.

* * * *

After they left her room, Kelly had lain across the bed. She didn't feel tired but fell asleep anyway. When she heard a knock on the door leading to T. J.'s room, she opened her eyes drowsily. She got up and slowly walked over to the door, then cracked it open to look through with only one eye.

"What?" Her voce was raspy with sleep.

"It's after five. We are going out to dinner, so get dressed."

"I thought I couldn't go out."

"We'll be with you, and I don't think we'll be running into any masked stalkers uptown. Plus, I'd think you might want to buy a few things to wear on the plane and on the island."

"Really? I get to go shopping?" she asked cautiously.

He laughed. "Yes, sweet pea, you get to go shopping. Now, go get dressed."

She closed the door and wondered what got into him. The man could be so confusing. He had called her sweet pea, and he had laughed and looked almost boyish. She ran into the bathroom to take a quick shower and to change. If she was going out into civilization again, she had to look her best.

Both Daniel and Taggert were waiting in the hallway when she came out. Danny gave a low whistle to her blue denim body suit with the zipper up the front and her black-heeled boots. Kelly gave a little mock bow and hooked her arms through those of her bodyguards.

"I must be the luckiest girl in uptown tonight, being escorted by two big dashing men."

Daniel puffed up his chest. "Yeah, that's me, dashing. Let's leave the lieutenant. You and me, we could go dancing."

"Aw, Daniel, we can't leave poor Taggert behind. Besides, you wouldn't be able to keep up."

Taggert played along, teasing lightly. "Very funny, you two. Now be good before I leave you both at home."

"I'll be good, daddy," Kelly said in a cute, little girl voice.

"Tell me that later, and I'll show you how daddy can be," he said softly just for her ears alone.

His words made a sexy tingle run through Kelly. She could feel the dampness settle against her panties. She wanted to see what "daddy" could do and show him what a naughty little girl she could be. The three of them walked out the double doors of the hotel, arms still linked, into the chilly night. Uptown Charlotte was filled with lights and passing cars.

"What are we doing first food or let Kelly go shopping?"

"Well, Dan, my man, how about we let the lady decide."

Both looked at Kelly who had already decided. "Shopping first, boys. You'll need dinner when I'm done."

"That sounded a little ominous," Taggert remarked.

"Be afraid, T-man. A woman shopping is like a hunter stalking prey."

* * * *

Both men soon found out that Kelly was like a tornado when it came to stores. After spending two hours in a place called Shoe Warehouse and then another hour going from store to store looking for her outfits, it was after nine before they sat down to eat. The highlight was when Kelly was picking out bathing suits. Because all were on sale since summer was over, she picked out three. Taggert could hardly wait to see her in the red high-cut bikini. He didn't tell her, but it was his favorite of the three. With their hands filled with her shopping bags, they squeezed into a booth at Morehead's Pub and stuffed the bags wherever they could.

"My God, woman, do you think you bought enough stuff?"

"Daniel, I just bought essentials for the trip."

"I think it's enough for two trips."

"Well, Taggert shouldn't have offered if you two were going to gripe about it."

"Hey now, I'm not griping. It's the detective over there."

"She didn't hear you grumbling behind her, that's why, Taggert," Danny said mimicking the way Kelly said his name. T. J. rewarded him with a kick under the table.

The conversation was cut short by the waitress arriving to take their order. Danny looked at the voluptuous woman with new interest. He watched the sway of her hips as the waitress walked away. "I think she added in a bit more oomph just for my benefit."

"Come on, man, put your eyes back in your head," Kelly said snapping him back to the table.

"What? Hey, I was just observing."

"Uh-huh, you were two steps away from drooling. You know she might have a brain, if you decided to find out what is above her neck."

"Yeah, Danny, have some decorum," T. J. said jokingly enjoying watching Kelly chastise his friend.

"Why T. J. when Kelly was looking at bathing suits you seemed none too interested in what she was thinking." Danny's voice had become southern syrup. "As a matter of fact, I recall you saying something about the red bikini and her firm—Ouch!"

* * * *

Kelly watched but said nothing, wondering what was firm on her that Taggert wanted to see. She made a mental note to wear that red suit as soon as she could. Throughout dinner, the banter and playful mood remained. The men helped her to relax and forget her troubles. Being in a booth with Danny and Taggert flanking her, she felt secure like nothing could touch her when they were around. Her gaze met Taggert's every now and again, and she saw something different there. She smiled at him on this occasion when their eyes met, and she saw a flare of passion in his. It startled her, and her body hummed in anticipation of things to come. The threesome got back to the hotel after eleven, carting Kelly's purchases up the elevator and to her room and depositing them on the floor unceremoniously.

"Hey, hey! Watch the merchandise!"

Danny looked at the bags on the floor. "I'm watching them. Are they supposed to get up and dance?"

"Smart-ass. Get out of my room, both of you," she said pushing Danny to the door.

"Oh, baby. You do make 'ass' sound so nice with that accent. Say it again," Danny teased.

"Goodnight, Daniel." She laughed while closing the door on his grinning face.

"Does that mean me as well?" T. J. asked quietly.

"Yes, you too. I have a lot of packing to do."

"Is that the only reason?"

"Yes—I mean no." With a sigh, she looked at the man who made her want to melt into her shoes with one touch.

"I don't understand you, Taggert. One minute you are ready to jump my bones, then the next you're cold, telling me that's against the rules. I-I have to think because this time if I jump head first into the pool, I might drown."

T. J. said nothing as she spoke, as her words trailed off. He walked toward her. He slid his hands around her, one around her waist and one cupping her neck. They felt strong and warm against her skin and through the material covering her back. She closed her eyes as the sensation flowed through her.

"No, look at me." His voice rumbled out, low and sexy.

She opened her eyes languidly. They felt heavy as if she was on some sort of a drug.

"When I kiss you like this, is there any doubt of what I want?" He trailed kisses along her bottom lips, biting its fullness gently. He pulled her against him, his breath tickling her ear and he spoke, "You feel how hard I am for you, Kelly? Does that feel like a man who doesn't know what he wants?"

He licked her ear, and she shivered in pleasure. She felt the wetness dampen her, and she wanted to take everything he offered. This time she had to let her mind win and not listen to her body or her heart. This time she had to play it safe.

"Say yes, Kelly," Taggert whispered against her lips.

"No," she moaned out softly.

"Yes?"

"No," she said again more firmly and pushed out of his arms, even though she wanted to be lost in them.

"No, Taggert, I can't. I have to think, and I can't do that when you touch me like you do."

"Then don't think."

"I have to, for my sake I have to so just go to bed and . . . just go to bed, Taggert, please," she implored.

Taggert took her into his arms once again and kissed her gently. "Okay, I'll go. See you in the morning, Kelly."

"Goodnight, Taggert."

"I'll leave the door unlocked in case you want to cuddle or anything else," he teased.

Her response was to throw a pillow at the closing door. Kelly threw herself on the bed, looked up at the ceiling, and let out a deep breath. Lord, she wanted that man. She sat up for a moment, rethinking her decision and then rethinking it again. Instead, she began going through her purchases and packing her things for the trip tomorrow. She stopped her folding and stared at the door dividing them. She wondered if on the other side of the door, Taggert's body throbbed as he got ready for bed. Was he lying in bed aching for her as well? She closed her eyes imagining he lay in bed under the blanket, his hand against the bulge in his pants, hoping to relieve the pressure. Were lingering thoughts of how her body felt against him and how her nipples pressed against her top making him ache? She couldn't wait until he had her under him panting and begging for release. With that thought in her head, she flopped onto the bed, pulled a pillow over her head, and groaned in agony. Sleep would be impossible tonight.

* * * *

He sat alone in his special room. His immortality seemed in question. He wondered if he had played the game too long. Like a cat playing with a mouse before eating his prey, did he let this one get out of his grasp? Kelly, his beautiful dove, had gone underground. He had spent all day looking for her with no success. None of his usual connections had known anything at all. Not even the redhead lady cop from Greywood's precinct knew anything. Even Greywood had gone missing.

The word was that the stress of the case made him take an unexpected leave. *So they want to play it that way,* he thought angrily. *Now they all have to die.* And Kelly, he would make sure she felt pain before she gave him his priceless treasure. None of the others had run. They had not fought against their destiny, but she had been corrupted by the lieutenant. Now she would have to feel his wrath. His choir had gone silent. There was no beating of hearts surrounding him, and they were disappointed in his efforts to find the last. He fell to his knees with tears streaming down his face and pleaded for them to understand, promising them he would find her, the last piece. Then he raged at them cursing them, for being silent when he was the powerful one. He promised them torture and suffering for Kelly Justine.

Then slowly, as if they were appeased, he heard one thud then another, then another. Soon the choir sang again, louder than ever, letting him know that they believed in him, that he was their savior. Kelly, his dove, would be found. He just had to wait for a sign. They were stupid, would leave tracks, and then he would be there. There was no more time for dalliances, no more killing just for fun. Well, maybe after his ascension. But for now, he had a mission, a task to complete. Kelly's heart would be his. He would take it from her chest while it still beat. He'd watch her blood spill between his fingers and would listen to her screams while he did it. He sat back in his chair, waving his finger to a melody only heard in his head from the hearts he had so mercilessly cut from his victims.

Chapter Ten

The plane to New York was surprisingly empty, yet Kelly sat between her two companions. The stewardess looked at them curiously, and Kelly smiled to herself, imagining how one small woman between two large men looked. The captain's voice came on the loud speaker telling the passengers of the flight time and other pertinent information. Kelly barely listened. After a restless night, she was tired. She had been very aware of the man in the other room, and no matter how she had tried, she could not get her mind to shut down so she could sleep. Now Taggert sat next to her, so close she could feel the smoothness of his leather coat and smell the spicy cologne he wore.

As the plane took off Taggert reached over, clasped her hand, and pulled it back onto his lap, holding it there. Kelly just let it be. It felt nice to hold his hand, and she rubbed her thumb against his.

Two and a half hours later, Gem Airline flight 477 took off from New York's JFK airport heading for the calm island of Barbados. This flight was also very empty, partly because it was a night flight and partly because the tourist season was over. Again, Daniel and Taggert flanked Kelly. She had fallen asleep about an hour into the flight, half listening to Danny flirt with the exotic stewardess and half listening to Taggert playing with his BlackBerry. By the time she woke up, her head was against Taggert's shoulder, and he and Daniel were in conversation.

"I'm telling you, T. J., if I could hook up with this stewardess on the island, it would be sweet."

"Danny she probably flies regular flights. Besides, I thought you were living with someone."

"Yeah, she broke it off. She wanted more of a commitment and me working fewer hours. Now I'm free and single and ready to mingle with the island girls," Danny said mimicking what he assumed was a Barbadian accent.

With her eyes still closed, Kelly said, "That's a Jamaican accent, us Bajans do not sound like that."

"Thought you were sleeping, island girl?" Taggert remarked.

"I was until Mr. Daniel over here decided to start destroying the lingo."

"Hey, mon, I visiting the islands, mon," Danny said again.

Kelly sighed. "Why do Americans always assume that island means Jamaican?"

"What's the difference?"

"Listen and learn, Danny boy, listen and learn."

Kelly pressed the call button, and soon a beautiful, dark-skinned stewardess appeared. Taggert and Danny listened as Kelly's voice changed from soft sultry British to exotic Barbadian in an instant. She asked for a drink and inquired about how much longer they would be in the air. By the time the conversation with the stewardess was over, they'd found out that there was about an hour left of flying and they both grew up around the same area of the island and knew some people in common.

"See. Now that's the difference between the two dialects," Kelly said smugly.

Daniel sounded almost sad. "But your British accent, it went away."

"It always does when I go to the island. Remember I was born there, lived part of my life there, so it's still in me, plus the British. When I'm home, I'm Bajan gal with a twist."

"Now I have to go potty, so let me pass, you big brute, and leave the poor girl alone."

She waited as Danny got up to let her pass, and she walked down the aisle to the bathroom. "Wow she's something isn't she"? She heard his comment as she walked down the rows of seats.

* * * *

There was a knock on the bathroom door as Kelly was fixing her makeup.

"Occupied," she called through the closed door, but the knock came again more insistent.

She sighed in frustration. Cracking the door to tell the person to keep their shorts on, she met the gray eyes of Taggert looking back at her.

"Taggert, what are you . . ." she said, then gasped as he pushed his way in and forced her to step back.

"Let me in quick before someone sees."

"Taggert, this is the restroom! What are you doing?"

He stopped the stream of words with a hard kiss, taking her lips and forcing his tongue in her mouth. When he released her, both were panting from the intensity of the kiss.

"Do you know how sexy you sound when you do the island girl voice?"

Kelly tried to clear the cobwebs the kiss had created. "Is that what this is about?"

"Say my name, but like you did before."

"Taggert, this is crazy. Someone might want to get in here, and I must say, this is a little kinky. Not that I'm complaining, mind you."

"Then say it," he coaxed.

Kelly decided to play along and slowly drawled out his name.

His hand slid up her thigh and cupped her ass. His eyes had gone dark to a smoky gray. "Again," he commanded.

Kelly did as she was told and repeated his name. His hand came around and slid between her panties touching the part of her that was already wet. She gasped his name, and when he took her mouth in a searing kiss, he slipped his fingers deep inside her. She was already slippery wet, and he moaned into her mouth when she contracted around his fingers.

Taggert sat on the toilet as she stood in front of him with her legs spread and her chest heaving with every breath. She was past caring where they were. She needed to feel his hands on her. Looking into his eyes, she unbuttoned her shirt exposing her breasts to him. When he pulled the cups of her bra down, the twin globes spilled out, the rings she had through them glinting under the fluorescent lights. He caught the nipple between his lips, and she arched in pleasure.

"Oh, Taggert, touch me again please."

"Where, baby? Where do you want my hands?"

"Between my legs, like before. I love how you touch me."

He obliged her and slowly rubbed his fingers over her swollen clit. He felt her buck and spasm against him. With his mouth he suckled her nipple deeply switching from one to the other. Her taste was intoxicating him, he felt like he could swallow her whole. He worked his fingers deeper inside her, watching as her head tilted back in ecstasy and little moans escaped from between her lips. She moved her hips against his hand, trying to get more of his fingers, and gripping his shoulders, she rode his fingers. Tension was building in her, threatening to consume her.

"Taggert please, I-I can't." She almost sobbed it felt so good. She didn't want it to stop.

"Yes, you can, baby. Come for me, yes," he groaned.

She began to shake, and her scream was silenced as he took her lips. She convulsed around his fingers again and again, could hear him through her haze of pleasure until she collapsed weakly against him. She kissed his neck as T. J. held her until her body quieted, and she lifted her head from against him.

"I'm sorry, Taggert, so sorry," Kelly began to apologize trying to regain her composure.

She could feel her embarrassment fill her face with heat. She had not meant to go out of control like that. She moved off him quickly, trying to fix her skirt and her blouse in the process. T. J. stopped her hurried movements and held her face in her hands.

"What are you saying sorry for?"

"This, I didn't mean to lose it like—like that."

"Let me ask you, does that always happen?"

Kelly sighed. "Not always, not for a while. Only when it's intense, and not for a long time."

"When's the last time?"

"Jeez, Taggert, I'm embarrassed enough as is. Fine, almost a year ago," she admitted.

He gave her a big hug and a kiss. "Don't be sorry or ashamed of your response. I liked it, a lot. Never been with a girl who was multi-orgasmic. You're amazing."

"Okay, but what about you? You didn't, well, have release," Kelly said.

"Don't worry, sweet pea, I intend to get mine where there's more room, and you're horizontal."

"Now let's get you cleaned up and looking like you weren't just ravished in the plane's bathroom."

A few minutes later, Taggert walked out first, and then Kelly behind him. Luckily, the airplane was almost empty and the other passengers were asleep.

"Taggert, want to know something?"

"Hmm, what?"

"When I'm horizontal, it gets way more intense than that." With a swish of her soft skirt, she passed him in the aisle and went back to her seat leaving him staring after her.

Danny stared at her when she came back and sat down, and then, a minute later, stared at Taggert when he waltzed up behind her. Taggert looked smug like the cat that ate the cream, and Kelly looked flushed and glowing. Danny screwed up his eyes and then said in disgust, "Aw, man, you two make me sick. On the plane?"

"I don't know what you're talking about, Daniel," Kelly said primly.

"And I plead the fifth," Taggert added.

"Whatever," Danny said. "Just don't let me see."

"Thought you wanted to watch, Daniel," Kelly said cheekily.

At his horrified expression, she began laughing.

* * * *

Gem Air landed in Barbados at three-fifteen in the morning. The air was chilly when they crossed the tarmac to the airport. The wind rustled the lush leaves on the trees that surrounded the airport.

"Doesn't it smell great?" Kelly said inhaling deeply, the scents of ripening fruit and sea air assaulting her.

"Ummm, it sure does," Danny said, and Taggert nodded in agreement.

Customs was a breeze at that time in the morning, and soon they were driving down the coast in the rental car that was waiting outside. Out the window of the SUV, they could see the moon hanging low over the sea, the waves rolling in on the dark beach, and the lights from the various hotels dotting the shoreline.

"So where are we staying, T-man?"

"In St. James Parish, in a guest house right on the beach."

"That's where all my family is!" Kelly said delightedly.

"That's why I picked it By the way, your brothers should have already opened it up for us and said they'll see you in the morning."

"Taggert, when did you speak to my brothers?" Kelly asked suspiciously.

"Before we left Charlotte, and before you ask, they don't know about the trouble yet. I told them you were coming home for a visit."

"They didn't question you about who you were?"

"They did, but I told them we would explain when we got here."

"Uh-huh. It would have been nice if you told me that you spoke to them."

"I would've eventually. Oh, by the way, they said to tell you a family party will be held. Before that we'll fill them in."

"What-What? Taggert!" Kelly sputtered, unable to find words to explain her frustration. Her parents in New York didn't even know. He'd already talked to her brothers and was planning to form her family into his private little army, without speaking to her.

In the seat next to Taggert, Daniel was laughing at Kelly's outraged expression and Taggert's innocent look. Danny tried to soothe her. "Kelly, it's no use. When the lieutenant here has to handle things, he gets them handled."

"But my parents don't even know, nor my sister, and . . . and he talks to my brothers who'll call my parents. Then I have to explain why I didn't tell them, because I didn't want them to worry. You don't understand how my family works."

T. J. glanced in the rearview mirror at Kelly, whose face looked like it was ready to crumple into tears. "Okay, babe, I told your brothers not to mention anything to anyone that you were coming for a visit. So before we talk to anyone, you can call your mom and dad in the morning and fill then in before anyone else."

Kelly relaxed her breathing and tried not to panic. That sounded reasonable. She'd tell her parents first before the rest of the family knew. "Just don't make any decisions about my family without my knowledge or consent, okay?"

"Gotcha," Taggert agreed. "I feel like I'm talking to a lawyer all of a sudden—'knowledge or consent,' you can be so formal sometimes."

"I went to an all girls Catholic school, what do you expect?"

"So you wore those little plaid skirts and knee socks . . ." Taggert's words trailed off, and a wide smile spread across his face.

"What are you smiling about?" Danny asked. "Oh, yeah, mental image forming as we speak."

"Hey, my image, buddy. Think about something else."

"Both of you are nuts," Kelly said, looking at each of them.

"Here we are, The Pearl Beach Guest House, right on the lovely sand of the St. James coast with its own wading pool directly into the crystal blue sea," Taggert announced pulling into the gravel driveway.

"Very nice. It's absolutely marvelous," Kelly gushed.

Taggert puffed up his chest like the ringmaster of a three-ring circus and boomed out, "We have three bedrooms, two bathrooms in a limestone-built house, full patio with a hot tub outside on the deck."

"No need to sell me the pitch, I'm sold," Daniel commented. "I've decided to give up this silly life of being a cop and to move here to fish all day and dance all night."

Kelly laughed out and even though it was the middle of the night grabbed the hands of both men and pulled them outside. "Let's go see the beach and the sea."

They walked off the patio, passed the lighted hot tub bubbling with steam rising in the cool night air, and stepped onto the white, fine-grained sand of the beach. The smell of the surf assaulted Kelly as the waves crashed gently onto the shore. Even in the middle of the night, the scene was breathtaking, shadows of the coconut trees against a midnight blue sky.

"Gosh," was the only word Taggert could manage.

Danny managed a nod of approval, and Kelly only sighed as they stood there and stared out at the beauty that surrounded them. Kelly felt at peace. Calm settled over her as if being back in her homeland made everything okay. She was aware of the man next to her, the one that had found his way into her life, and having him there made this homecoming seem even more special.

"Okay, guys, let's go get some sleep and see what the day brings us," Taggert said.

"I want the bedroom that faces the ocean," Danny said calling dibs.

"It's the sea," Kelly corrected him. "The Caribbean Sea, remember that, big guy."

"You don't have to call first on the bedroom, Dan, my man, the perfect thing about this house is that it is built with all the bedrooms facing the ocean." Taggert corrected himself after seeing Kelly's raised eyebrow at his last word. "I mean the sea."

"Good. Now let's get some sleep so I can get up and go look at the locals cavorting in the nude."

"Not in this life, Daniel, but you keep dreaming." Kelly laughed as they headed up the stairs.

They took the same sleep arrangements as they did in the hotel, Kelly's room in the middle flanked by both men. They each went to their own room with the exhaustion of the day settling in. Kelly looked around her room. A huge mahogany canopy bed sat right in the middle with gauzed lace encasing it like some whimsical dream. To one side, the fabric was tied back so she could get into bed. There was a small knock against the door, and she walked over to answer, knowing instinctively that it was Taggert. He stood there with a white hibiscus in his hand.

"This is for you," he said handing her the bloom. "Welcome home."

"Thank you," she said softly. She lifted the flower to her nose and inhaled its exotic scent.

"Would you like to come in?"

"Not tonight. When I come into your room, it will be when you are sure and ready, not half dead on your feet. The plane was just the first part of what I want from you," he said with a boyish smile on his face. "But I will take this," he added, then claimed her mouth in a soft kiss. Tenderly their lips rubbed against each other causing such wonderfully erotic friction. Her eyes fluttered open when he drew away from her.

"Don't look at me like that. I might forget I'm trying to be noble."

"Like what, Taggert?"

"Like I'm the only man in the world right now. Goodnight, Kelly," he said, walked a few steps down to his room and went inside.

As Kelly closed the door to her room, she leaned against the cool surface and put the flower to her nose again. "Maybe in my world you are," she whispered.

She was too tired to do anything else but slip out of her clothes and put her hair into a ponytail before climbing into bed. The sheet's pristine white was cool against her skin and the sounds of the surf lulled her into a drowsy state. *You love him you know,* her heart whispered. She couldn't deny it, she loved Taggert. Her problem was not loving him but letting him go when this was over. Her love couldn't make him stay. His job would be over regardless of the outcome, and Kelly didn't know if she could handle the goodbye.

* * * *

T. J. sat up in bed. The thought that just hit him shot through him like a cannon, and he sat there staring at nothing, the sheet falling down to his waist exposing his hard chest. He loved Kelly! *Damn, this is what love feels like.* He had thought he had been in love a few times, but this was unlike anything he'd ever experienced. He rubbed his hand over his chest where his heart beat against his hand. *Good going, you fool, now you've gone and fallen in love,* he thought.

Shit, what was he going to do now? He lay there, staring at the ceiling trying to figure out what came next, what to do, how to fix it. Nothing had come to mind even as he drifted off to sleep with Kelly's face in his thoughts.

Chapter Eleven

The morning dawned clear and blue on the island. Wearing only a pair of jeans, Daniel stood on the deck looking out over the sea. He hadn't slept long, only about three hours. By the time he woke, it was already seven a.m. The first thing he had done was to walk out and take a deep breath. Now he looked at the boats dotting the horizon. Some were closer to the shore, and he could see fishermen casting their nets for the day. Even though they were here for a dangerous reason, that he could feel so light and at ease was amazing. He turned around as he heard the sliding door open, and T. J. padded out barefooted and bare-chested too.

Danny turned back to the view in front of him. "Isn't this a sight, man?"

T. J. stepped up beside him. "That it is."

Just then, two ladies in tiny bikinis ran by, their skin glistening in the sun from their early morning exercise. They waved, and T. J. and Danny lifted their hands to return the wave and watched the pair as they went out of sight.

"Now, that's what I'm talking about," Danny said with a big grin on his face. "Did you see that, T-man?"

"Yeah, T-man, did you see that?" The soft voice belonged to Kelly, and when they turned, they saw the smile on her face was wide and bright.

"See what?" T. J. said innocently.

"Uh-huh. So you're saying that you weren't watching the two bouncing bikinis running down the beach?"

"Depends on how long you were standing there."

Danny piped up. "Hell, I'll admit it. I was watching the bouncing bikinis."

Kelly's laughter flowed. "Come on in and I'll make breakfast Bajan style. My brothers stocked the place with everything I would need."

"Sounds good to me. I'm freaking starved, must be the sea air," Danny said as he passed through the patio door.

* * * *

T. J. looked at Kelly as he passed through the sliding door. Seeing her smile falter, he wondered what she was thinking that caused her smile to fade. They both watched as Kelly mixed up something called "bakes." The mix was simple just flour, water, sugar, cinnamon, nutmeg and black essence. T. J. found it strange they were called bakes when they were fried in a pan with oil. He mentioned it, and she gave him a look that meant don't ask dumb questions, so he settled back to wait to see what they would taste like. For the first bite, he took half of one of the small cakes that reminded him of fried muffins. Danny didn't seem to mind. He wolfed down three before Kelly knocked him on the hand with a spoon and told him to wait. Then she went on to make fresh sausage patties, eggs, and thickly sliced bacon wrapped in white paper so T. J. knew they came from a butcher. To top it off, there was fresh mango juice and coffee. Danny's smile grew as she put each dish in front of them. Needless to say, Kelly found out, as he had when they had served together, that Danny loved his food.

She watched Danny eat. "How do you put all that in there and not gain weight?"

Danny replied around a mouthful of food, "High metabolism."

T. J. laughed at Kelly's expression of amazement. "We used to call him 'packer' when he was in the military, 'cause no matter what it is he was eating, he could pack it away."

Even T. J. was amazed at how Daniel packed it away this morning. There was a knock on the sliding door, and Kelly squealed in pleasure. She rushed over and was enveloped in hugs by who T. J. assumed were her three brothers. From living in the sunny climate, the three men were a little darker than Kelly. They could have been linebackers in a football team, and their size made the kitchen seem smaller.

"Taggert, Danny." Kelly was breathless between laughing and being squeezed.

"These are my brothers, Maxwell, Anthony, and Timothy."

The brothers repeated the shorter version of their names to T. J. and Danny.

"Max."

"Tony."

"Tim."

"Hi, I'm T. J., and this is Danny." T. J. introduced them both while Danny just waved, his mouth full.

There were handshakes all around, and the men sat down and began eating breakfast as if they had been there all morning. T. J. looked at the siblings. The brothers were huge compared to Kelly's tiny figure. All the men wore their hair in braids that went down their backs, and he could see some resemblance around the eyes and lips, but that's about where it ended.

"So, Kellybear, what trouble have you gotten in this time?" Tony asked.

"Kellybear?" T. J. choked on his juice, and Danny hid his smile behind a napkin.

"Yeah, she always insists on calling us by our full names so we made that up for her when she was ten," Max said.

"It stuck, the whole family calls her that," Tim added.

T. J. looked at the three men and Danny, and between the four appetites, there was nothing left on the table. Luckily, he was full.

"So who's the oldest?" T. J. asked.

"I am," Tony responded. "Then Max and Tim. Kelly pulled up the rear."

"We could not get her out of our hair," Tim said.

"Remember the time she got stuck in the mango tree."

"Shut up, you guys," Kelly warned.

"Oh yeah, we wouldn't get her down, and she shimmied down and her shorts got caught on a branch," Max added.

"And to get down she had to shimmy out of her pants and run into the house in her bloomers," Tony ended the story.

T. J. was laughing until his eyes watered, and Danny could hardly contain himself.

"Oh, we have to hear more about Kelly in her wild child ways," T. J. said wiping his eyes.

"We'll get around to that, but we need to know what's up, Kelly." Tony said.

"I'll fill you in." T. J. began the tale of what Kelly had been going through with the killer stalking her. By the time he was finished recounting the events, her brothers' faces had turned hard as stone and looked as deadly as some of the jagged rocks around the island. "That's why we brought her home. We figured better to hide in plain sight, but around her family, that way we'll know whose out of place," T. J. finished off.

"Oh, we'll know who's different. We know these beaches and the regulars around here," Tim said.

"Anyone messes with Sissy here is going to get fucked up in a bad way." Max's face was cold and angry as he spoke.

"Don't worry, Kellybear, we got you now girl." Tony took her hand and squeezed.

Kelly got up and hugged each of her brothers. "I knew that I only had brothers for a reason."

"So now breakfast is over, let's hit the beach," Danny said, pushing away from the table.

"You like jet skies or wind surfing?" Max asked.

"Both," Danny answered.

"Good. We rent the water equipment out on this beach so it's on us," Tony said.

"Okay. I'm going to run up and change, and I'll meet you guys on the beach." Kelly pushed her chair back from the table. "And call Mom and Dad to let them know what's going on."

"Do that, Kellybear, before Aunt Mauve gets to them first," Tim said.

The group of five watched her go up the stairs, and then Tony turned and looked at T. J. "How bad is this, man?"

Her brother's eyes turned to him and waited for an answer. "It's bad. I've got to tell you reality is totally lost on this person, but until he makes a move, we can't do anything. For at least a few days, she can relax and take it easy, but when he gets here, we have to be on alert. We can't make a move unless he does first, even if we find out who he is." T. J. explained hating that they could do nothing before this maniac made his presence known.

"That's fucked. If we know who he is, we can't go bash him?" Tim asked angrily.

"No. He has to make a move on Kelly first," Danny said quietly. "I know what you guys are feeling. I think of Kelly like a sister myself and I want to hurt this guy bad."

T. J. wanted to do the same thing as well, but he knew that to catch this guy, they had to go about it the right way.

"We'll fill the family in before you get to the house tonight, but we'll leave out some of the more serious stuff. We don't need Aunt Mauve doing one of her fainting spells in the middle of the party," Max said.

"They're fake," Tim said with a chuckle.

"Now, let's go see what trouble we can get you guys into on the beach. Then tonight we'll show you how to party, Caribbean style!" Tim slapped his hand on the table.

"That's what I'm talking about," Danny said. "Let me ask you, how friendly are the women?"

Daniel talked with Max and Tim as they walked away onto the beach, leaving T. J. and Tony alone.

"T. J., you can go on with them. I want to talk to my sister a minute alone, okay?"

"I prefer to wait," T. J. said protectively.

"I'm her brother, man. I'll get her down there safe. I've kept her safe all her childhood."

"Yeah, but I've been keeping her safe now." T. J. knew he sounded belligerent but could not help it.

"Okay, but I'm still her big brother, and you brought her home for us to help," Tony responded unfazed by T. J.'s tone. "I like you, T. J. So far what I see you are a good guy, don't make me beat you up."

T. J. grinned. "I could probably take you. I am military."

Tony laughed. "Yeah, but I wouldn't go down easy, and I could probably beat the hell out of you before I did."

The men formed a friendship then and there over threats of violence and the need to protect Kelly.

"I'll see you down there then," T. J. said and walked off, leaving Tony alone in the kitchen to wait for his sister to come down.

* * * *

Kelly came downstairs to find her brother Tony sitting alone at the table. He looked up as he heard her footsteps coming down.

"What are you still doing in here, Anthony?"

"Waiting for you, baby sister." He looked at her fondly.

For an instant, her mind flashed to when she was a child running around with her hair flying and free. Being the only girl, she had always had a special bond with her brothers. Tony and she had been more alike than the rest, and that had created a special bond between them.

"How are you really, Kelly?"

Kelly sat down, took her brother's hand, and sighed. "I'm scared, terrified actually. This man, whoever he is, has a target painted right on my forehead."

"He isn't going to get at you," Tony said.

Kelly had missed the rich, thick accent from her brother and impulsively got up and hugged him. "Thank you, big brother, but everyone keeps saying that and he's still coming."

"Trust us. That T. J. guy looks like he knows what he's doing," Tony commented.

Kelly hoped that her expression did not change at the mention of Taggert's nickname. She said softy, "Yes, he knows what he's doing. If it weren't for him, I'd probably be dead by now."

"You got that look, Kellybear. What's going on with you two?"

"Nothing, everything. I really don't know, Anthony."

"Ah, I see. You got feelings for him, eh?" Tony looked directly at her.

She could feel him scrutinizing her. Kelly looked at her brother and admitted for the first time to anyone. "I love him."

"Does he love you?"

"I don't know. Let's not talk about it now. Let's go outside. I finally get to enjoy the beach."

The finality of her tone told Tony it was the end of the conversation, so he got up. "All right, let's go, Sissy. See if you can remember how to run the "cat."

The shortened named for catamaran reminded Kelly how much fun she had growing up helping her brothers run their rental shop.

"Oh, we'll see all right, race ya there!" she shouted, already through the door into the sunlight. At only nine-thirty in the morning, the sun was already hot and the beaches filling up with tourists.

"You always cheated," Tony called out to her as he ran after his sister.

* * * *

T. J. immediately spotted Kelly running between the people milling around down the beach. Her hair was loose, and she wore the red bikini she bought in Charlotte. The rental shop owned and run by her three brothers was a stone's throw away from the guest house. It did not take long for T. J. to catch up to Danny and her other two brothers. Danny was already out on the crystal blue water on a jet ski, and already there was a hot little number riding on the back. T. J. could see his grin from the beach, until Kelly took his attention away. The red bathing suit showed off her every curve, and he could see other men on the beach looking in her direction as she ran passed. Out of breath and smiling, she stopped directly in front of him in a flurry of sand.

"So how do you like it so far?" she asked, winded from the sprint.

"Okay, you win, sis. I'm going to go bring the cat out," Tony said and walked off holding his side.

"You'd think he'd have caught me," Kelly said, looking at her brother walk up to the rental shop aptly named Just Jammin'. "So you never answered, Taggert, how do you like it?"

"It's fine. Hot and the water looks great. Danny's already out on the water." T. J. added, pointing to where Danny was making figure eights in the surf.

Kelly waved to him, and he waved back. "Who's the girl?"

"I have no clue. He was talking to her on the beach, and next thing I know she's on the back of the jet ski."

"That's Sue. She works for us now," Max said. "Remember Ms. Tully who lived down the road from us? Well, that's her daughter."

"That's Sue!" Kelly exclaimed. "Um . . . she's grown. She is four years younger than me, and now she has a lot of . . . um, assets." Kelly looked at the girl hanging onto Danny tightly.

"T. J., you want to take the cat out with me?" Tony said pulling the light craft down into the sand.

"Sure why not. Coming along, Kelly?" T. J. asked.

"Not yet. I'm going to take a swim and lie on the beach for a bit."

With that, Kelly walked down into the water until waist high and then dove beneath the cool surface. When she came up, the water glistened and clung to her skin. She wiped the hair off her face and then languidly floated.

"You will have to help me pull this thing in the water," Tony said, watching how T. J. was looking at his sister.

"What? Oh yeah, right . . . sorry." T. J. held onto the rope of the other end and began to pull alongside Tony.

"Your mind was somewhere else, eh?" Tony commented with a wide grin, and then the two of them pulled the craft into the water and climbed on.

T. J. didn't bother to answer. He sat back and watched Tony fix the rope, and the breeze took the sail and pushed the catamaran out into the open water. Tony showed him how to work the sails and how to keep the craft gliding smoothly. Soon, T. J. was handling it on his own and enjoying himself to the fullest. It had been a long time since he had taken anytime off from work to relax even though he was still on the job. This helped him relax in the midst of all the chaos they had to face. The two men sailed for about an hour getting to the cliffs that buffered the north side of the island before turning around to go back to the beach from where they had set off. They neared the shoreline, and T. J. could see Kelly lying on a beach towel on the sand. Next to her sat a buff blond guy, and they were having a conversation. T. J.'s mouth tightened, and he narrowed his eyes. He scanned the beach for Danny and saw he was not too far away sunning himself. His gaze shifted back to Kelly and the guy sitting too close to her. When his fingers touched the spots on her back, T. J. was off the catamaran and into the knee-deep water in an instant, moving quickly toward the pair.

As T. J. walked up, the guy touched the tattoo on her back again.

"What's going on here?" he growled dangerously.

"Taggert! Hi. Nothing's going on. This is Sam. He's visiting here from South Carolina. Do you believe it, we're neighbors."

"Really, what do you do, Sam?" T. J. asked quietly.

Sam with the blond hair and rock-hard abs said, "I'm a model, we're here on shoot. I was telling Kelly her tats are original, they're cool."

"Telling her and touching her are two different things, Sam," T. J. bit out.

"Taggert! Don't be rude," Kelly said in shock at the tone T. J. had taken.

"Hey, Taggert is it? I was just talking to the lady."

"Number one, no one calls me Taggert. Two, if you touch her again, I'm going to beat you over that pretty model head with your own arm. Go away, now." The menace in T. J.'s voice was undeniably clear. He didn't give the model a second look as he got up and moved away quickly. T. J. was focused on Kelly.

"We're taking the cat out, Tony," he called pulling Kelly along with him.

"Alright."

"Get your big mitts off me, Taggert. I'm not your property, and you can't— Hey!" she cried out as he picked her up, put her on the craft, and launched them out of the low water.

As T. J. pushed the small craft out into the water, he saw Danny walk over to where Kelly's brother stood. He heard their conversation while he was getting the last of the weighted ropes that kept the catamaran from floating away.

"The guy's got it bad for your sister man," Danny said

"Pity he don't know what to do about it," Tim teased back, knowing full well T. J. could hear everything they were saying.

They all laughed, and the men gave Danny a serious look before Max said, "Seriously man, if he hurts her, we'll have to kill him and feed him to the sharks."

Danny took them seriously for a minute until they started laughing once again.

Oh, I know what to do about it, T. J. thought as he pulled himself out of the water and onto the boat. Amid their laughter and Kelly's tirade, the boat sailed out into the open water.

* * * *

Kelly sat in the middle of the cat fuming. *How dare he act like a big brute, scaring the poor guy, then throwing me onto the boat and sailing out.* T. J. could feel her hot gaze burning into his back. He sat there, taking the craft far away from the shore then he dropped the small anchor to hold it in place.

He turned to her then and she started in on him "How dare you, you son of a-a—I won't even say bitch because I like your mother. You drag me off like some bloody caveman and sit there saying nothing. Say something!"

"You are so hot when you're mad," he said simply.

With a screech, she threw herself at him, and in trying to hold onto her, they rolled off the boat. Kelly came up sputtering and wiping the water from her eyes. T. J. surfaced with a smile on his face. Both were treading water and staring at each other. Then he pulled her close for a long kiss.

Licking the water from her lips, he said, "Salty."

"Why'd you act like that, Taggert?"

"He touched your skin, and I wanted to break his fingers. All right, I was jealous, I admit it. Okay?"

"Okay," she said and pulled him in for a kiss.

Her tongue met his in his mouth, and the kiss went from soft and tender to hot and deep. Kelly wrapped her legs around his waist, leaving it to T. J. to keep them afloat. They went under the water for just a moment, lips still locked in a kiss. They came up, and T. J. pulled away.

"Baby, baby," he said against her lips. "We've got to get out of the water before we drown."

"We won't drown."

She slid her hands down his stomach and directly into his swim trunks taking hold of his manhood. He was smooth and hard like velvet against steel. T. J. pushed himself against her hand.

"I want you, Taggert. No more waiting, now."

"Jesus, Kelly, are you sure? Lord, tell me you're sure."

Kelly swam around to the side and pulled herself up. By the time T. J. followed her into the boat, she was gloriously nude, her bathing suit off.

"I'm sure," she stated and held out her hand to him.

She watched T. J. slide his trunks off and come willingly into her waiting arms. They lay there on the soft mat of the boat, the waves moving the craft in a gentle motion and the warm Caribbean breeze caressing them. He trailed his lips down her neck, biting her gently, and Kelly gasped in excitement before he licked his way down to her voluptuous breasts. He suckled her dark, large nipples until she could not help but writhe beneath him.

"Taggert, please now. I want you inside me," she moaned. The sun kissed her skin on the outside, but inside, she was melting at her core from the feel of his touch.

His cock pressed against her. She could feel him probe her wet entrance, and she opened her legs wider in invitation. As he filled her slowly, she watched his eyes fill with pleasure. Kelly wrapped her legs around his waist and raised her hips to meet his slow, sensual thrusts. With every movement, she caressed the hard muscles of his shoulder. She took him deeper. The ecstasy of having him inside her sent her passion higher. She knew he was keeping his pace slow to hold himself back. He wanted to give her his all before he found his release, and her heart filled with indescribable love for him. Her moans were long and sexy, like a cat purring, and her head moved from side to side.

"More, baby, please more," she begged as he took her nipple gently between his teeth.

T. J.'s breathing became harsh as he tried to control himself. "What do you want, Kelly? Tell me."

"You, Taggert. Only you. Give me more." She moaned, pulled her legs back so he fit more deeply inside her, and was lost in the sensation. He slipped his hands under her and pulled her tighter against him. She felt T. J. let go of all restraint and give her what she needed, what they both needed, hard and fast as they moved in unison.

Fisting her hands in Taggert's hair, Kelly felt her control slipping. His words made her burn so hot she couldn't catch her breath.

"Look at me. I want to see you come for me."

She opened her yes and saw him above her like Adonis against the sun. She pulled him in for a kiss. Her body tightened around him, and then with a low cry, she reached the flashpoint of fulfillment. Taggert pressed kisses onto her lips and neck. He let himself go cresting where she had been a few moments before filling her with part of himself. As moments passed, they lay still wrapped in each other's arms, neither needing words, only to feel each other.

When she felt him watching her, her eyes opened and saw him resting on his elbow.

"Are you okay?" he asked.

"I'm fine. I'm wonderful actually," she said, smiling at him.

"I'm sorry that it was here. I wanted it to be more romantic," he began to explain.

"There is nothing to apologize for, don't ruin it by saying sorry."

"No, I will never be sorry. I just wanted to give you something special before—"

"Before what, Taggert?"

"Before we get this all settled, before we go back to our normal lives."

"And I'm not going to be included into your life when we go back to Charlotte?"

"It's not that simple. All this could be because of the emotional roller coaster you've been on."

Kelly asked slowly, "So my feelings can't be genuine because of my emotional situation? So what are my feelings?"

"I don't know, but we have to assume they are because of us being in such close proximity for the past few weeks. It's only a logical conclusion."

"Then let me tell you what I'm feeling, Taggert. I love you," Kelly shouted angrily. "With everything I have in me, I love you even when you are being an ass like you are now." Hurt and anger now replaced the sweet sensuality of being with him. "How dare you tell me what I feel and try to make it a logical conclusion. If you hadn't noticed, I don't live logically, and my feelings cannot be ruled by what you assume is logic. Can you say you love me? Can you look me in the eyes and love me without thinking this through like a soldier?"

"I don't know, Kelly. I can't do that. I have to think."

"Well, if you have to think, then it's not a love I want. I loved you without even knowing I did, and when I figured it out, I accepted it. Now I'll have to accept that my love is not returned." She dove off the catamaran and began to swim for shore, cutting through the water like a knife.

"Kelly, wait!" T. J. called after her.

But she wasn't listening. Kelly let the hurt running through move her through the water and across the beach to the guest house. When she whipped the sliding door open, there were tears streaming down her face.

Danny looked up from reading the paper with a glass of juice in his hand. "Kelly, your brother said to be at the house at eight." Then he saw her expression and came toward her. "What's wrong?"

Kelly swiped her eyes and tried to smile seeing the concern on Danny's face but her voice cracked when she answered him. "Eight, okay. I'll be ready, um . . . I'm going upstairs, Daniel, to take a nap and relax for a while, okay?"

"Kelly."

She was already backing up the stairs and waved her hands to ward him off. "I'm fine, Daniel, really. I'm tired, just tired."

She ran up the rest of the stairs and slammed the door to her room.

* * * *

Three days. It had taken three days to find out where they had taken his dove, but his persistence had paid off. This time he had to use an extra resource, a private eye who owed him a favor, to find them. He'd found out about their flight to Barbados and that the lieutenant had used his military ID to get through security at the airport. They were idiots—all of them—for thinking he couldn't find them. What did they think going there would do? Put him off his task just because she went home?

He packed for his trip, taking care to hide his tools in between his clothing knowing the bag would not be searched by airport security. The lieutenant thought he had pull, but *he* had so much more. He thought briefly that it might be a trap, but he shrugged that off as ridiculous. The two didn't have enough intelligence between them to come up with any solid theories, let alone plan a trap. That he would kill her where she was born was a sort of poetic justice. A fantasy of him taking her heart in a lush, green forest surrounded by rich vegetation and colorful flowers flashed in his mind. The air would be sweet, and the smell of her warm fresh blood flowing into the ground and soaking into the earth would make it sweeter. He felt himself get hard at the thought, and he opened his pants to relieve the excitement. He jacked off to the image in his head of killing her, of her blood smearing the petals or the flowers surrounding her. He felt his release against his hand as he thought of holding her still warm heart. He rested for a minute letting the images fade from his head slowly, savoring it. Then he got up, fixed his immaculate uniform, and walked out the door locking it behind him. He got into his car to head for the airport. His flight would be leaving in an hour and he had to stop overnight in Miami. It was the only flight he could get on short notice. Maybe after he took Kelly's heart and killed her two bodyguards, he'd take a vacation. His transformation would be complete by then and he could play with the ladies on the island. He could introduce them to his kind of play and maybe make a few videos to remember them. Ah yes, a vacation sounded like a good idea.

Chapter Twelve

Danny was still sitting facing the door when T. J. came in a half an hour later. It had taken time to put the boat away and lock the door like a note left at the rental shop said. The brothers had already gone. It seemed working for yourselves and on an island was easy, just make your own hours. By the look on Danny's face, T. J. figured out that he'd seen Kelly when she came in.

Danny exploded as soon as T. J. came through the door. "What the hell, T. J. What did you do?"

"Not now, Danny, I'm not in the mood!" T. J. barked.

"Well you better get in the fucking mood. You didn't have to be the one sitting here seeing Kelly running in crying!"

"She was crying?" T. J. asked softly. He ran his hands through his hair and sat down heavily.

"Fuck yes, she was crying, she could hardly get words out!"

"Shit!" The expletive was spit out of T. J.'s mouth. "She said she loves me, Danny."

"And what did you say to make her cry?" Danny asked sitting down as well.

"I told her it was probably because of the situation that we were in."

"When was this?"

"On the boat when we went out, after we, well . . ."

"T. J., for a man with twenty years under your belt in the military and so much intelligence, you're an ass."

"Danny, don't—"

Danny cut him off, "No, for once in your damn life you're going to listen. I've known you for what fifteen years on and off?"

T. J. nodded and Danny continued. "In that time I've seen you in battle, at funerals, and off the job. I've seen you with women and I've seen you without. You're stubborn and arrogant and goddamn cocky at times. But for some reason, she saw something under your prickly exterior and fell in love with you."

"Is that a round about compliment, Dan?"

"It wasn't meant as one. I'm saying that you are a lucky son of a bitch to have someone like her love you."

"She's messy," T. J. said looking for an excuse, any excuse, but for what, he didn't know.

"But she cooks like a dream," Danny countered.

"She's pierced in places that you wouldn't believe. She dances and sings for no reason. You've seen her place, it's decorated like a fairy castle mixed with a boudoir. She turns cartwheels on the lawn and feeds my dog potato chips."

"Well let's haul her down here and have her shot," Danny said sarcastically.

T. J. rolled his eyes. "I mean she is so unlike me."

Danny said, "The girl is a firecracker. Opposites attract. You can't even keep your eyes off her half the time." Danny leaned across the table. "Do you want to be with someone like you or someone to add pizzazz to your doldrums of a life?"

"I have to think about this, Danny."

"Your problem, T-man, is you think too much."

Danny left then and went upstairs leaving T. J. sitting at the table alone with his thoughts.

* * * *

Upstairs, Kelly had lain across the bed berating herself for telling Taggert she loved him. She had turned over, hoping that sleep would claim her, but her thoughts were on the man she loved. She wouldn't be chasing him anymore. She had bared her soul to him, and he had told her it was just a reaction, like love was some sort of allergy. If he wanted her, he was going to have to claim her, and this time she wouldn't be easy to catch.

After Kelly rose from a restless nap, she dressed carefully for the night's party carefully applying her makeup so any evidence of her crying could not be seen. She dressed completely in white. The short sheer dress clung her body.

The only color was a red sash that was tied high under her breasts, making them look fuller and exposing more cleavage. The red flower tie she tied her hair back and the white stilettos on her feet complemented the outfit.

When she came down the steps, a "va-va-voom" from Daniel greeted her. She smiled at him. "I take it you like the outfit?"

"You're lucky I'm not on my knees panting like a dog."

"You look beautiful, Kelly," Taggert said, looking at her.

"Thank you, Taggert." She walked past him and turned to Daniel. "Coming?"

Danny passed Taggert and lifted his eyebrow at him, which she pretended not to see, and T. J. followed them out the door. The drive to Kelly's family home was done in silence. She sat in the backseat, looking out the window and the passing coastline.

Taggert pulled the SUV into the long driveway with rows of lights that led up to a beautiful old plantation. It was the traditional white with shutters done in a hunter green. Plants and flowers were everywhere. There were orange trees on the lawn, and stringed lights in every tree they passed. People were already milling around, and the music filtered into the car.

"You lived here growing up?" Danny asked. "Lucky devil."

"Yup, I've climbed every one of these trees at least twice." Kelly smiled wistfully remembering how she had grown up feeling the grass under her feet and the smells of the island in her nose.

T. J. parked the car, and people crowded around. There were at least eighty people present.

Kelly got out of the car. "I'm home! Let's carnival!"

A cheer rose from the crowd, and Kelly was embraced and passed on from person to person, saying hello and kissing cheeks while Taggert and Danny stood by. They were not alone for long when Kelly's brothers flanked them.

"Come, have a drink. She'll be at this for a while." Tim led the way to the bar set up on the huge patio.

"Well, who these boys?" asked a large woman with a thick accent who had waddled up to T. J. and Danny and was looking them up and down.

"These are the guys that came home with Kelly to keep her safe," Tony replied to the woman who seemed to be the matriarch of the family.

"T. J., Danny this is Aunt Mauve."

"Nice to meet you ma'am," T. J. said and Danny echoed the same thing to the woman peering at them owlishly.

"Seems to me if Kelly was home in de first place she wouldn't need protectin'," Aunt Mauve said.

Kelly walked up at the end of her aunt's speech. "I love you too, Auntie."

"Humph, you was raise cheeky and spoiled rotten."

"Yes but you did most of it, Auntie." Kelly gave the older lady a big hug.

"Shoo way, let me go, crazy girl. Go enjoy yourselves all of you. Eat, drink, and dance, and I'll watch," said Aunt Mauve.

Danny grabbed Kelly's aunt's plump hand. "Oh no pretty lady we are going to dance."

The older lady fluttered her hand against her chest and twittered like a small bird "I like this one, Kellybear. Come, young man, let we cut a rug."

Off Danny went and soon was encased in a throng of people who were dancing on the grass. Kelly glanced at T. J. and then turned her back to him and went to the bar. She sat there for only a minute and drank three glasses of homemade rum punch. She didn't even look at him as she walked off the patio and began to dance with her family and friends.

As the night went on she laughed and talked with people. Every time she caught T. J.'s gaze she had a glass of something in her hand and made sure her laugh was just a little louder. The music turned to a slow reggae beat. It was the same song that had played when T. J. had eaten dinner at Kelly's apartment, that first time she had made him dinner.

T. J. watched Kelly take the hand of the man she was talking with, and they walked to where everyone was dancing. He had been on the beach before. Tony told him that the guy had come from Germany on vacation and never left, making the island his home. He was big and built like a Viking with dark hair, and his hands rested on Kelly's hips while she swayed to the music. She threw a glance over her shoulder to see T. J.'s dark gaze on her and her dance partner. Her movements were slow and sexy, the muscles of her body moved and flexed as she rolled her hips. She looked at the guys and smiled. Then she turned so that her butt pressed against him. She moved again encouraging him to catch the rhythm with his hips.

T. J. still gazed at her, and she played it for all it was worth. Kelly took the big guy's hand, placed them around her waist, and continued dancing. It was wrong she knew to take pleasure in seeing him angry at her action. But T. J. had hurt her and she wanted to hurt him back just a little. He crushed the frail plastic cup in his hand, and the liquid inside sloshed out. He stalked over to the bar to get napkins to mop the mess off his hands. By the time he looked back, they weren't dancing anymore but sitting on a piece of patio furniture with Kelly's feet in the guy's lap. At another glance over, she waved at Danny, who was now standing next to T. J. on the patio. T. J. mouthed, "Move," but she was too far away to hear what he said.

T. J. was not having it. She was sitting with that guy touching her, and all he wanted to do was to smash the guy's face in. He would do it too if the man's hand went any farther up her thigh. Then it did. Before he could move, he felt Danny's hand on his shoulder.

"Not here, man, not with her family around," Danny said.

"He's touching her," T. J. growled, his eyes barely slits.

"You know what you said to her. She's upset and more than a little drunk. Leave it be."

"If his hand goes any higher, I'll—"

"Leave it to her brothers," Danny finished.

"Don't look over there. Drink this and stay loose," Danny advised and handed T. J. a glass of something with a red tint.

But T. J. could not stop looking over at Kelly, who was laughing at something the bronze bastard said. How she laid her hand on his chest and listened to whatever he whispered to her while batting her eyes. The German man trailed Kelly's every move the rest of the night, and T. J. watched every step they took. Party-goers started leaving around two in the morning, and Kelly made her rounds saying goodbye to her family and close friends. T. J. and Danny said their goodbyes as well and waited by the vehicle for her.

"Did you enjoy ya'll selves?" Kelly asked, her accent thick slurred by the rum punch she had drunk.

"Yes, we did," Danny replied with a smile. "Why, Ms. Kelly, methinks you are sloshed!"

"Why, Mr. Daniel, you are correct!" She broke out in laughter while she climbed into the backseat of the car. Danny shook his head in complete amusement, but T. J. was silent.

On the way back to the guesthouse, they had to listen to her rendition of Bob Marley's "We Jammin" and other reggae songs coming from the radio. Kelly got out of the car and stumbled slightly on the stone steps. T. J. reached out to keep her from falling, but she pulled away from him and glared.

"Don't touch me, I'm fine," she snapped, continued on into the house on her own, and then up the stairs.

"Goodnight, Daniel," she called down, and he called up the same to her before they heard her door close.

"Yeah, you're in the doghouse big time, buddy." Danny chortled and slapped T. J. on the back.

"That's it," T. J. said quietly. He had silently taken her cold and angry stares all night. He watched as the German asshole had touched her, he drove home without uttering a word, and now his anger had reached its limit. He began to walk up the stairs.

"Yeah, I'll sleep down here on the couch," Danny called up the stairs to a silent T. J.

"That fine." T. J. knew he snapped at his friend, but he couldn't help it.

"T-man, a little advice from a friend who's had too much punch."

T. J. turned to look at Danny, who was standing with a sad but goofy smile on his face.

"Relationships . . ." he started with an amused snort. "Women and men are like gasoline and an open flame, but damn, isn't it fun when the explosion happens."

T. J. shook his head. "Uh, yeah. Goodnight, buddy."

He took the rest of the stairs two at a time and walked directly into Kelly's room without knocking.

"What in the bloody hell!" Kelly exclaimed. Her face darkened when she saw him. "Get out of my room, Taggert. You don't just walk in here!" she said angrily.

T. J. took off his jacket, threw it in a chair, and began to unbutton his shirt. "You spent all night ignoring me and dancing with that bastard," he said calmly. "You let him touch you."

"My body, T. J.," she snapped. "I do what I please with whomever I please to do it with."

"No you don't, not as long as you are with me."

"I'm not with you, you're little conversation took care of that."

He came to a stop in front of her and pulled her fiercely against him. "You're mine, Kelly, don't forget that."

She raised her eyes looking defiantly at him. "I'm not yours, T. J. I wanted to be, but no more."

"You said you loved me."

"I plan to cure myself of that condition," Kelly said.

T. J. slid his hands down her thighs and then up under her dress cupping her ass. Slowly he began to grind his hips against her. He felt her shudder and felt satisfaction in knowing she still wanted him.

"Did he make you tremble like this, Kelly, when his hands touched you?" T. J. asked fiercely.

"I was planning to find out before we came home, but too many people were around. But he did have a nice feel to him when we danced, full package of . . ."

She got no further. T. J.'s eyes flashed with anger at her last ditch effort to hurt him, and he shut her up with a kiss. There was no build to intensity, just an immediate burn. He dragged the tie that held her hair together out in one motion and grabbed fistfuls of her hair to hold her still as he devoured her mouth.

T. J. couldn't think. All he could do was feel her tongue duel with his and taste her while he sipped from her. He felt like a candle melting under its flame as her hands roamed over his taut body. T. J. cupped her breasts and pulled them from the confines of her dress. He buried his face in them before taking the hard nipple of one in his mouth and suckling deeply as if he were starving for her taste. Kelly cried out and arched, pulling him closer and offering him more of her.

"You taste so good. I can't get enough of you," he whispered harshly against her skin while licking and nipping her.

He worked his way back to her lips, and while he plundered her mouth, he untied the back of her dress. The scant material settled in a soft puddle on the floor, and T. J. lifted her and placed her on the bed. Kelly stared at him as he discarded the rest of his clothing and kneeled in front of her. With his hand at her waist, she lifted her body slightly when he took off her tiny pair of panties. He touched her in that secret place where she was wet and hot, his fingers traveling down the slit, while he watched her. She closed her eyes at his touch, and her breath slowly exhaled from her body.

"I'm going to taste you, Kelly," he said. "I wanted to taste you from the moment I kissed you, and I'm going to until you beg me to fuck you."

Her back arched, and T. J. heard her sexy purr as he lowered his mouth to her core. He held her when she bucked at the first lick, and when he delved his tongue into the secret folds of her body, she writhed. T. J. held her hips tight as he explored her with his mouth. Her hands were in his hair pushing him away yet pulling him closer while he took her to the edge. She moaned and begged for release, and then with a final flick of his tongue, T. J. reaped the reward her body had to offer.

Limp, Kelly fell back against the bed and tried to catch her breath from the explosive orgasm. T. J. was not done. He would have it all from her. Slipping one finger inside her while she lay there, he heard her moan. He slipped another finger inside, and he watched as her legs spread a little wider to accept what he was giving and her back arched in response to his touch.

"Do you like this, Kelly?"

"Yes," she whispered.

"Say that only I can make you feel this way," he commanded.

"Only you. Oh God, only you!" She panted as he pushed deeper inside her hot velvet box.

"Say my name. I want to hear you say it's only me."

"Taggert, it's you that . . . that makes me feel like this!"

"Good. Now come for me. I want to see you come again."

As if at his command, her body erupted again, tensing for what seemed like eternity. As sensation after sensation rolled through her, she begged him to take her with every breath that passed her lips. Watching her come was too much for T. J., he was hard to the point of pain. He needed to bury himself deep inside her. He got off his knees and slipped inside her. His groan matched hers as she took him in.

"I want to ride you," she whispered in his ear and nibbled the sensitive lobe.

T. J. felt himself burn at her words. He slipped from her wet body, lay on the bed, and watched her straddle him. She took his hard length in her hand and guided him inside her, taking him in inch by slow, torturous inch. He clenched the sheets in his hands as she rode him. He could feel her thighs against his as she moved and he watched her arch until her hair touched his legs. Sliding his hands up her body, he cupped her breasts and her pace increased. She took him deeper with every downward thrust. T. J. gritted his teeth and tried to hold onto her, losing all control. Kelly was past the point of reason, driven by that primal instinct to mate, to give and take pleasure.

"I need you, Taggert, I need you!" she cried out.

"I need you too," T. J. groaned. He meant it with everything he had in him.

"I'm going to come," she panted.

Taggert looked at her and saw tears on her cheeks. He felt the tightening of her body around his manhood. He knew she was going over the edge, and he let go. Both fell into the abyss that lovers find in each other.

Kelly was sprawled on top of T. J. The breeze coming through the window from the sea cooled and dried their skin. T. J. stroked the hair from her face and kissed the tears drying on her cheeks. She rolled off him and turned her back to him. Rolling over, he fit his body to hers and covered them with the blanket. He pressed his face into her neck and inhaled her scent. He thought he would never tire of how she smelled or how she felt in his arms. Kelly shook, and T. J. heard the small sob she was trying to mask by covering her mouth with her hand. He turned her to him and saw more tears, this time not from the pleasure of their lovemaking but of sadness. The look in her eyes made him want to kick himself for being the cause of it.

"Did I hurt you?" he asked softly.

Kelly tried to control her voice. "More than you will ever know."

It took T. J. a moment to figure out she didn't mean what had just happened.

"Kelly, I can't stand to be away from you, but I can't say what you need me to say."

"Do you thinks it was easy for me to fall in love or to give my heart to you," she cried. "There are things in here, Taggert, that a lot of people don't get to see. I'm not just the happy-go-lucky girl, and for the first time in a long time, I want someone to see what's inside me. That person is you!"

T. J. listened to her words and to how heartfelt they were. He loved her, he knew that, but the unknown terrified him, preventing him from saying the words. How could he say them if he didn't know it would last forever?

As if sensing his thoughts, Kelly caressed his cheek. "Sometime you just have to take a leap of faith."

She turned her back to him again, and this time, she pulled his arms around her, bringing his warmth close to her. He settled in behind her. He listened to her breathing slow to the relaxed state before sleep. Before she went slack, she whispered, "I love you, Taggert."

T. J. felt his heart respond where his mouth could not. That leap of faith was like a cliff in front of him. Did he dare to jump?

* * * *

A phone was ringing in his head. T. J. mumbled in his sleep and turned. His face was buried in Kelly's hair. The ringing was persistent, and he felt Kelly move as it broke though her sleep. After too much rum punch the night before,

T. J. imagined the sound of the telephone was like cathedral bells to her.

She poked at T. J. half heartedly. "Make the ringing stop before my head explodes. She swatted him on the head and pleaded. "Taggert, your phone, answer it."

"Regretting all that rum now, huh?" he mumbled.

"Answer your cell. If I get up, I'm going to break it."

"Grouch," he scolded before kissing her head, turning to the nightstand, and retrieving his cell phone.

T. J. patted her rump under the blanket as she buried her head under the pillow to block out the sounds of the cell and his voice.

"Hello, Lieutenant Chapel here." He adopted the brisk military tone he used at work.

"Lieutenant Chapel, we've got a hit."

Recognizing the voice of his trusted colleague Sergeant Holden, T. J. came awake instantly. They had left on Tuesday night, and it was Thursday morning. He'd expected at least a week to pass before the killer picked up their trail. Swinging his legs off the bed, he pulled on his crumpled slacks from the night before and walked out of Kelly's room and to his own next door.

"Tell me what you have, Holden," T. J. ordered.

"I'm faxing it to you now, but this can't be just a coincidence," Holden said. "I've put the name in the system, and so far, he's been stationed in every state the murders have been committed, and he is in Charlotte now. The reason we have pinned him is that he's high profile, sir. He's one of the guys they send in to form the new black ops task forces that infiltrate and destroy terrorist sleeper cells."

"Are you sure? We don't want to blame someone this high up without proof."

"I'm ninety-nine percent positive, Lieutenant Chapel. Every murder has happened around the time he's been to one of the states. His background lists him as pre-med before joining the service, and then he was a field medic overseas. He's the only one that has purchased a ticket and boarded a flight to Barbados in the last twenty-four hours."

"He could be on vacation?" T. J. said, not wanting to believe what he was hearing.

"Sir, he must have wanted a vacation pretty bad. The ticket he bought on Wednesday to travel the same day was twice the usual price, and it was a layover in Miami overnight. So he'd be arriving today at around noon at the Barbados airport. Lieutenant, sir, everything fits."

"Good job, Sergeant. What are you faxing me?"

"Sir, it's his military record, all the information I've compiled, and his picture."

"Okay. I'll look it over. Did you contact our superiors to give them the heads-up?"

"Not yet, sir. I wanted to speak to you first."

T. J. knew his men did nothing without his say so, were completely loyal to him, and would never go over his head. "Okay. Go upstairs personally and call a meeting ASAP. Tell them you are under my orders to do so. This does not go into a memo. And you run the brief. When everyone is gathered, call me on the landline and we'll confer on this."

Holden gulped in excitement and fear at having to brief the men upstairs. "Yes, sir. Right away, sir."

"Get the cops to get a warrant. We have enough probable cause to get one and get into his place."

"I want you there when they go in, and you inform me what they find."

"I'm on it, sir."

"Holden, before you get off the phone, what's the name of this guy?"

"Sir, it's Captain Jeffery M. Callister."

"Thank you, Holden. Get on with it," T. J. said and hung up the phone. He watched as the last piece of information fell out of the fax machine, and he stared at the picture of Captain Jeffery Callister.

Chapter Thirteen

So this is the bastard that is stalking Kelly, T. J. thought looking at the picture once more. He was what T. J. considered a pretty boy. With dark hair and green eyes, he didn't look like a military guy, and far less than one trained in secret infiltration and black ops.

T. J. changed quickly into a pair of jeans and a polo shirt. He looked in on Kelly to find she had gone back to sleep and he went downstairs. After putting on a pot of coffee in the kitchen, he walked through to the living room where the big man sprawled out on the couch was snoring, and shook him. "Hey, Dan, wake up. Duty calls."

Danny cracked open a bloodshot eye. "Crap, T. J., it's too early. I'm not in the barracks anymore."

T. J. snorted. "It's after ten, and this is important, so get your ass up. He's here, and we know who he is."

"Damn! I'm up, I'm up." Danny scrambled off the couch and moved quickly to the stairs. "Give me a sec to get on some fresh clothes."

"I'll be in the kitchen. Coffee'll be waiting."

Five minutes later, T. J. looked up as Danny came back down the stairs, taking enough time to throw on a pair of shorts and a T-shirt and to throw water on his face. T. J. could see by his expression that the party the previous night had taken its toll.

"Man, I feel like I did a few rounds with a bear," Danny mumbled as he sat heavily in the chair at the table. "Did you ever notice that the sun seems way brighter on this island in the morning?"

"Yeah, well, a light bulb would seem like the sun to you the way you drank that stuff last night."

"It's the devil's drink, I swear." Danny looked as innocent as possible while pouring a cup of coffee. "The damn rum punch might be sweet, but it packs a wallop."

"Yeah, yeah."

"Okay, so who is the scum, T. J.?" Danny took the first sip of the hot liquid.

T. J. slid the folder toward Danny. "Captain Jeff Callister, United States Army, over twenty years in. He was a Ranger, then became an instructor specializing in black ops, hand-to-hand combat, and infiltration."

"Fuck me." Danny whistled.

"You said it, man. Plus, he was pre-med when he joined up in eighty-one and a field medic his first year in. Christ, he's been in Columbia, Panama, Cuba, Lebanon. So much of the freaking Middle East. All black ops missions. The file has so many parts blacked out its like trying to read code.

"Field medic, pre-med, that's the medical angle we were looking for," Danny said still reading the file. "The man was every place there was a murder and they stopped when he left."

"He's on his way here. I've got my man setting up a meeting on my end and getting a warrant on yours."

"I'll call my captain to see how it's going and will get Kirk in on the warrant."

T. J. nodded. "Good. We'll have us a tight little net by the time we are done."

"Should we wake Kelly and let her know?"

"No, let's get everything together first and make sure we're on the ball. Then we'll let her know."

"You got it, T-man."

"By the way, from now on we're always armed. He isn't going to get a chance to catch us with our heads low."

"Hell, T. J., I'm armed now." Danny slipped his waist holder from his back and put his piece on the table.

Danny got out his cell and began dialing. Soon he was immersed in a conversation with his captain and his partner. T. J. was thinking how things changed from low to high voltage in such a short time. Yesterday they were playing on the beach as if enjoying a trip. Now they knew who the killer supposedly was. The first hard lead since the whole thing started, and everything kicked into high gear. He felt as if he was losing time. Soon it would be over, and he would have no reason to be at Kelly's side. Would he be able to face losing her or would he be able to admit his feelings and take that leap of faith she talked about. At the same time, the landline rang, and he answered. On the other end were Sergeant Holden and his four superiors.

* * * *

The conference call lasted for half an hour and his superiors were none too pleased with the latest developments. But they acknowledged that it was best to handle it quickly to keep the military from any more bad press. They gave T. J. their approval to do what he must to bring this to an end.

When T. J. walked into the kitchen, Danny looked up and signaled to T. J. that he needed one more minute to finish the call.

"Okay, Kirk, call me when you get in the house."

T. J. gestured to Danny that he needed to say something.

"What?"

"Tell your partner that Sergeant Holden is on his way there to be the rep for the army on this."

Danny relayed the information to Kirk and hung up. "The warrant is being written up as we speak, T. J. If there's anything there, they'll find it."

"Oh, they'll find it," T. J. said grimly. This was the guy they were looking for. His gut told him they were on the right track. "Until then, we wait."

"What then?"

"When they find the proof we need, we put the authorities here on alert and Kelly's brothers. If he comes we'll be waiting," T. J. replied. He hoped that this Jeff Callister put up a fight. He wanted to dispense some payback.

* * * *

When Danny answered the phone an hour and a half later, he could hear the horror in Kirk's voice.

"Dan, oh man! Oh shit!" Kirk repeated before Danny could get a word in.

"Let me put you on speaker phone, Kirk. Who's there with you?"

"It's me, Sergeant Holden, Charlie the coroner, and the SWAT team. Callister lives off Rea Road in a ranch-style house. The downstairs is fine, immaculate, but up here in the attic, he has a motherfucking shrine. It's where he keeps the victims."

"Describe what you see," T. J. ordered.

"First, he has a padlock on the door on the outside. In the attic, he had an old bed set up in the corner and a table at the bottom of it. The drawers have needles, tubing, and an assortment of surgical implements, scalpels, rib spreaders and the such. He has the water cooler bottles that Charlie said he thinks he used for disposing of the blood. But the sick fuck has a shrine with a chair in the middle of pedestals. On each is a jar with a human heart inside surrounding the chair directly in his line of vision."

"Jesus Christ!" Danny breathed.

"Charlie said that the one in front has to be like twenty years old. I think it's his mother's. There's a picture of him with a thin, older lady stuck under the jar. The word 'Matriarch' is written on tape and stuck to it. Jesus, Dan, he killed his own mother!"

Grimly, Danny said, "Thanks, Kirk. Get it all bagged and tagged for evidence. Seal that goddamn house up tight after the CSI is done. No one in or out. And put a car on it until we catch this fucker."

"Make sure that you get a copy of everything Sergeant Holden," T. J. added.

"Will do, lieutenant," the sergeant said.

At the end of the call, T. J. and Danny looked at each other in disgust, both knowing this guy had to be taken off the streets.

* * * *

It was after one before Kelly finally descended the stairs to find the men sitting in the kitchen with papers all around them. She yawned and stretched as she passed them and ruffled Daniel's hair. When she had woken up, the memory of the night before shot through her, and she decided to just let things lead where they may. If she got hurt, she'd have to pick herself up, dust herself off, and hope it didn't destroy her in the process. She loved Taggert, and she knew she would love him until the stars burned out in the heavens.

"Good morning, menfolk," she said. "I need coffee, that rum punch has fried my brain cells."

"Kelly, you need to come and sit down," T. J.'s said.

"After some coffee. I swear my family is crazy. Did you see my Aunt Mauve shaking her groove thing?"

"Kelly, come sit down."

She caught the tone in T. J.'s voice this time and knew that the person they had been waiting for had arrived.

"He's here, isn't he?" she whispered. Her hand that held the coffee cup shook and she had to carefully set it on the counter.

"He's coming, and we know who he is," T. J. confirmed.

Kelly sat down. "Who is he?"

"He is, like you first said, military. Captain Jeff Callister."

"Are they sure, are you sure?"

"They found evidence in his house, sweet pea. He had a little treasure box with pictures of his victims. They found a secret room in his attic. They found his collection of hearts. He keeps them in jars. Trophies." T. J. looked at her as he talked.

Kelly grew cold. From T. J.'s expression, she knew her face had gone pale, and she clasped her hands to keep them from shaking.

Danny spoke up. "He's already landed on the island. The authorities here called us when he came through customs."

"Why didn't they arrest him? You found the h-hearts and the proof. Why not just arrest him there?" she asked in an agonized voice.

"Because they have no authority to. They are, in essence, back-up for us. He has to come for you so we can take him." T. J. explained calmly. "If he knew for an instant we are onto him, he would disappear. He knows how."

"They were following him, but they lost him, and now we don't know where he is," Danny told her quietly.

"How can they lose a guy on the smallest island in the whole chain?" she cried out. She calmed her breathing, letting out a slow, deep breath. She felt like running, but to where, she didn't know. She tried to speak as calmly as possible. "So now we wait for him to make a move."

T. J. nodded. "We wait, but anywhere you go outside of this house, Danny or myself will be by your side, and your brothers will be watching the beach."

"They know?"

"They were here when you were sleeping," Daniel answered. "We showed them who they should look for."

"You have his picture, can I see it?"

T. J. turned the folder to her, and she finally looked at the face of the man who had terrorized her days and made her nights filled with nightmarish dreams. The cold green eyes that she remembered from the first night stared out at her from the picture that lay on the table.

* * * *

He was on the island, finally. The layover in Miami had been excruciating, and he had hardly slept. Now he was in the midst of the lush tropical paradise. When he left the airport, he had noticed the two policemen following him. In their gray uniforms with a red stripe down the side, they stood out from the tourists. He figured they thought he was running drugs or something illegal, so he quickly lost them on the trip to where he would be staying. He paid the cab driver with the dreadlocks an extra U.S. twenty dollar bill to take the scenic route. The man's eyes lit up with the twenty waving in his face so he took the route from the airport that lead through St Thomas and the gullies it was known for. Jeff Callister made mental notes on everything he passed. He fell in love with the gullies especially. The cabby was as happy as a clam to tell him all the information about the surrounding areas. The little tour was very informative, and he had already decided that one of these gullies would be the place he took his final prize. Now it was just a matter of finding Kelly. The research he'd done on her had her family being situated in St James Parish, where her brothers owned a business. The cabby knew it, seemed everyone on the island knew of the business since it was the best and on the busiest part of the island for the tourist sector. He passed the rental store on his way to his accommodations and decided he would lay low tonight and tomorrow start his reconnaissance. There would be a way to get her, he just had to watch and wait.

* * * *

After the talk she had with T. J. and Danny, Kelly's nerves were frayed to the limit. She could not keep still. She had cleaned the kitchen, the living room, and the upstairs, and even after that, she could not relax. Deciding to cook, she got started, and once she started, she created a feast. T. J. was sitting in the living room in front of the TV when Danny came downstairs and passed through the kitchen. He looked at Kelly with her full concentration on cooking. She didn't even look up to pass him a silly comment. Danny sat next to T. J. on the couch.

"Uh, what's she doing out there?"

T. J. sniffed the air. "Smells like beef stew, homemade bread, and brownies." After he sniffed the air once more, he added, "Oh, and pound cake."

"Wow, she's cooking up a storm."

"She does that when she is stressed. You should taste some of the stuff she made at my place."

"Are you going to talk to her?"

"For now, no. She uses this as catharsis. I'll wait until after dinner," T. J. said.

T. J. heard Danny's stomach rumble. He looked at T. J. when he raised an eyebrow. "Hey I haven't eaten anything all day except a few cookies out of the bag and a can of soda and it didn't seem the same after eating her cooking.

'Uh-huh." T. J. grinned as Danny's stomach rumbled again. "What's living in there?"

"Did she say when it would be done? I'm starved."

"I never noticed how much you eat, Dan. She didn't say when it would be done."

"I'm telling you now, T-man, if you get stupid and leave her alone, I'm going to have to marry her just for her cooking."

T. J. grunted knowing he was thinking the exact same thing a few weeks ago. They sat in the living room watching the cable news, and Kelly continued her culinary meditation in the kitchen. Soon she came out, dusting her hands on her apron that happened to cover a tank shirt and a pair of cut off shorts. T. J. thought there could not be a more alluring sight.

"Hey, guys, dinner is done if you want to eat." She was subdued and quiet.

T. J. could see that this man, this Jeff Callister, was drowning her spirit with just the thought of his presence looming over her.

"Great, I'm wasting away here," Danny joked.

Kelly barely smiled as they settled in the kitchen. She served the men and herself and placed the fresh baked bread on the table with butter. The smell had both of the men's mouths watering, and they dug into the food eating with relish.

"This is amazing, sweet pea. Thank you for dinner."

"Yeah, thanks, Kelly," Danny echoed before shoveling another spoonful of the rich stew in his mouth.

"You're welcome." She sat there pushing her food around and taking very small bites.

T. J. knew she hadn't eaten all day. "Aren't you going to eat?" he asked her gently.

"I am, I am." She put a spoonful of the rich stew in her mouth. He saw her take a few more bites and take her plate to the sink.

"There's a lot left if you want any more," she addressed the two men. "Brownies and cake too. I'm going to go upstairs for while."

* * * *

She didn't even wait for a response. Kelly just went up the stairs quickly and shut the door to her room. Even though T. J. and Danny were downstairs, she had this need to lock the doors and windows and never leave the room. A knock on the door startled her, and she had to press her hand against her lips to stifle the automatic scream that welled up in her throat. T. J. walked in holding a small plate with two brownies and a glass of milk.

"Thought you might want dessert."

She smiled. "I made it, remember?"

"Yeah, well, you ate like two bites of food."

"I'm not really that hungry, Taggert, but thank you."

He set the dish down on the table and sat beside her. "Come here," he whispered' and she went willingly into his strong embrace.

"Will I ever feel safe again?" she whispered against his chest. "I feel so cold, like I'm lost, and I don't know how to find my way."

"Baby, I swear to you, you'll feel safe again. When he isn't in the equation anymore, then you'll feel safe again. Until then you lean on me, sweet pea." He kissed her hair.

"I don't want to lean on you, Taggert. Don't make me need that."

"Why?"

"Because when you're gone, then I'll fall."

"I won't let you fall, Kelly," he said, not understanding the full meaning of her words.

"Not on purpose, not on purpose."

They sat in silence for a while, and then T. J. kissed her impulsively. "Come on, I know what will make you relax. A dip in the Jacuzzi out there."

"I don't know . . ." she started hesitantly, not wanting to be outside.

"The warm, bubbling water relaxing your muscles," he coaxed. "Don't worry, baby, we'll be right there with you. Go put your swimsuit on."

"Okay," Kelly got up and went to the bathroom to change.

* * * *

"I'll be downstairs," he called through the bathroom door and heard her muffled response. He went and put on his swim trunks before heading back downstairs. When he entered the kitchen, he found Danny fishing around.

"Danny, you can't be still hungry?"

"Growing boys need their food. I have a taste for something sweet."

"Do you eat like this at home? And by the way, you're thirty-seven, you're done growing." Under his breath, T. J. added, "Or at least I hope so."

Danny grinned. "I heard that. Where you off to? Night swim?"

"No, we're going to sit in the Jacuzzi for a bit, see if it helps her relax."

"So that means you talked and it's okay?"

"I don—"

Danny made a frustrated sound under his breath. "Forget I asked. You know, time waits for no man. I'll be in the living room in front of the tube." Danny walked off with three brownies on a plate, then turned back to the refrigerator. "Forgot the milk."

As he walked off, T. J. shook his head in bemusement and then went into the refrigerator himself and got a bottle of wine he had been chilling. With that and two glasses in hand, he went out to the deck where the Jacuzzi bubbled and the lights cast a sensual glow. He got in the warm water and lay back against one of the jets, letting the tension ease in his back. He closed his eyes and opened them quickly when he heard soft footsteps on the wood floor. Kelly stood there wrapped in a burgundy bathrobe.

"Don't just stand there, hop in," he said with a smile.

Kelly looked around hesitantly as if expecting Jeff Callister to jump out of a piece of shrubbery at any second.

"It's fine, Kelly. I promise no one's here." He inclined his head again to invite her into the swirling tub.

With just a nod, Kelly slipped the robe off and laid it across the lounge chair. T. J.'s breath caught in his throat as she turned to him. The one-piece bathing suit was black against creamy chocolate skin. The cut was high against the thigh. The bathing suit itself was of am intricate weave across her body leaving sexy swatches of skin exposed and a neckline that plunged almost down to her navel.

"Damn," he said between his teeth. He thanked the heavens he was immersed in bubbles. Just one look at her in that suit gave him an instant hard-on. Kelly slipped into the Jacuzzi next to him and let the water come all the way up to her neck.

"Isn't that nice? Was I right about it relaxing you?" He wanted so much for her to relax and be at peace in the midst of the terror.

Kelly looked at the hopeful expression on his face and smiled. "It's wonderful, Taggert, you were completely correct."

He laughed. "I love when you get all perfect English on me with that prissy accent. It's adorable, Kellybear."

"You're not allowed to call me that, Taggert," Kelly warned.

"Why not? It's so cute. Kellybear. You call me Taggert."

"It's your name. That is not my name, just the product of teasing brothers."

"I like it, Kellybear."

She narrowed her eyes at him. "You'll pay the consequences if you do that again."

He leaned forward until he was nose to nose with her and whispered, "Kellybear."

Kelly splashed him with water, and while he wiped his face, she dunked him under the rippling water of the Jacuzzi.

T. J. came up sputtering. He glowered at Kelly, who was laughing at him and pointed. "It's on, little girl."

"Now, Taggert, think about this. I warned you about consequences and look what happened." She tried to explain, and when his expression told her it wasn't working, she tried an apology.

"I'm sorry, Taggert," she said as solemnly as she could and tried to look remorseful.

"Oh, it's past sorry, sweet pea."

Kelly squealed and tried to run as T. J. lunged for her. He caught her around the waist, pulled her back into the hot tub, and dunked her.

It was she who came up this time gasping and wiping her hair out of her face.

"Taggert!" she wailed.

"Hey, fair is fair, baby," he drawled.

They stared each other down as if in a wild west shootout and then the splashing began, each trying to splash each other as much as possible. T. J. ended the game by grabbing her up in a bug crushing hug, laughing right along with her. She wiped the water from his face, and he kissed her soundly on the lips.

"Damn, I love you, girl," he said as he rested his forehead on hers.

Kelly's eyes flew open, and she stared at him. "Did you say what I think you just said?"

There was no point in denying it. It had come out as naturally as breathing. He loved her, and he would spend the rest of his life loving her.

"I meant it, sweet pea. I fell in love with you from the first moment you called me Taggert in stead of T. J. My heart knew it, but my head just took a little longer to catch up."

She kissed him once, then twice, and again for good measure. "Taggert, you think too much."

He chuckled against her lips. "You know I've been told that a lot lately."

"So where do we go from here, my sexy beast?" She nibbled on his ears and that soft spot on his neck that she had discovered made him shiver.

"Upstairs if you keep that up."

"Mm, sounds good, but I meant with us?" She continued to nuzzle his neck.

"Why, Ms. Justine, I just might have to marry you when we get back to Charlotte."

She got out of the Jacuzzi slowly, and he watched the rivulets slide down her body.

"Well, you'd better or Danny promised to marry me just for my Chicken Cacciatore."

When he growled at her, she squealed and ran into the house and around the kitchen table dripping wet. T. J. came running in after her grinning from ear to ear.

"Hey, hey, hey, what's going on?" Danny asked from the entrance to the living room.

"He's going to marry me!" Kelly giggled and squealed again as T. J. made a grab from her, and then she dashed off upstairs.

"Damn right I am," he yelled up after her. T. J. shot Danny a wide grin and thumbs-up sign before bounding after Kelly, both leaving drops of water and wet footprints across the floor in their wake.

"About freaking time!" Danny yelled up behind them.

* * * *

Out on the water, a small boat sat bobbing in the calm water. In it sat Jeff Callister with a pair of high-powered binoculars to his eyes. He saw the play in the pool, the intimate kisses and caresses, and the mad dash to the house and upstairs before his detective counterpart locked up and walked back to an inner room he could not see. He was absolutely livid. The fucking lieutenant had touched his prize, his dove! He would pay. They would all pay! She was a whore, a slut. She knew she belonged to him, yet she let him fuck her. He should go in there right now and kill them all, bash their heads in until they could not be recognized, then burn the house with them in it and watch until everything including them was ashes on the ground.

But not yet. He could not go into this without a plan. He needed her heart, which was of the utmost importance. How he took it from her, and the amount of agony she felt, was up to him. He would make her suffer before cutting the heart from her chest. He planned to muffle her screams and to watch the tears roll down her cheeks from the pain. He'd make her pay until her eyes begged for forgiveness, and then he'd take his prize from her. He scouted his target, knew the paths he needed to take, and all he needed was the opportune time to pluck her from the lieutenant's grasp. This time, the dove would be his.

Chapter Fourteen

"It's been four days, Taggert. Can we please go somewhere?" Kelly complained.

"No, around here is fine. We can't go anywhere with him lurking around."

"But we haven't seen him, not even once. Do we even know if he's still on the island?"

After four days of nothing from Jeff Callister, Kelly was getting antsy and her need to be doing something bubbled up to the surface. T. J. tried to keep her occupied over the last few days, but now nothing could keep her settled.

"He's still here. He isn't going to leave without trying. He's waiting for us to make a mistake."

"Danny, talk to him. Tell him we can go somewhere other than the beach and the rental shop," Kelly implored.

"T. J.'s right, Kelly. He's waiting for us to make a mistake."

"Wasn't the whole point of this little excursion for him to try to get at me? If you keep me where he can't, this will never end. How long can we stay away from home?"

"She has a point," Danny commented.

"Pick a side, will you?" T. J. hissed at Danny in frustration.

Danny held up his hands as he leaned back in the chair. "You both have valid points. We need to keep her safe, yes, but we can't sit here forever. We have to get out there, give him an opportunity to make a move, then grab the asshole."

"Great use my future wife as bait," T. J. bit out.

"We were going to do it before you figured out she was your future wife."

The serious tone Danny had made T. J. look up. Under the jokester and the eating machine he knew Danny was all business. Trained to kill or be killed at one point and using what he knew to find and put away the scum that frequented the streets or Charlotte.

Kelly placed her hand on T. J.'s cheek caressing it gently and he kissed her palm. "I can't hide forever. I have to take my life back if we're going to have a life."

T. J. sighed heavily, knowing they were right. To catch Jeff Callister, they would have to get out into the open. "I guess we're going sightseeing today."

Kelly clapped her hands and smiled. "I know the perfect place to go. It's the best tourist attraction in Barbados. We're going to Harrison's Cave."

An hour later, they were changed and in the car, with Kelly sitting in the front seat giving T. J. directions to the cave. They drove through the capital of the city called Bridgetown, where all the storefronts were done in beautiful colonial buildings. The vendors on Swan Street tried to sell their wares, yelling out prices for fruit and souvenirs, to capture a few buyers. They stopped for awhile roaming the different little stores selling sweet smelling oils and crafts. Tourists were buying fresh fruit to eat and coconut water to drink while they roamed the clusters streets.

* * * *

Amid the people clustered on the small streets with cars, minibuses, bicycles all moving slowly, trying to get somewhere or do something, the group did not notice the man following them. Jeff Callister had come prepared. He had brought a wig in his luggage, had gone to the extreme of shaving off his mustache after he had arrived, and wore thick lenses now. Following them cautiously, he blended with the crowd. Any time one of the three looked behind, he paused as if he was shopping like the other tourists, even, on occasion, buying a few things that would look nice in his special room when he took his prize home and to remind him of the special way he had taken it on the island.

He watched them walk back to the car slowly, and he, too, strolled casually toward the Jeep he had rented days before. He watched them drive off with Kelly laughing as the wind whipped through her hair. *Soon her laughter will turn to screams,* he thought with anger. Following a few cars behind them, he watched as they turned onto the road that led to where his fun would begin.

Harrison's Cave was located in the middle of the island in the parish of

St Thomas. The wondrous cave held its own beautiful, naturally formed rock formations that seemed as if God had molded them like clay from his own hand. A giant waterfall splashed into a pool of clear spring water the size of a giant swimming pool and held its own natural hot spring. The cave itself was massive, and to take the tour, tourists had to ride a trolley-like vehicle on electric rails. The lieutenant, the detective, and his dove arrived as the second tour for the day was going into the cave. It would be at least an hour before the trolley came back for the next tour, which included them. Until then, one of the many tour guides invited the tourists to look through the visitors' section and the gift shop. He watched, feeling such glee that none of them even knew he was there.

It couldn't have gone better then if he'd planned it himself. He'd seen them drive into the entrance of the cave tours and had taken another turn, one toward the gullies next to the cave. *Do they think I'm not planning my next move?* He was a soldier for goodness sake. He'd gotten in and out of some of the most dangerous countries in the world without a scratch. This was a piece of cake for him. He parked close to the second entrance he'd found to the cave. He doubted that the Barbadian people even knew of this entrance. Scouting the area one night, he had come across it. There under his manmade camouflage, he had hidden some essentials he needed. It was just one of four little stashes he had hidden. He walked through the dense underbrush and made his way through the small opening to the cave he found. Some of the cave was not lit or finished with construction for touring. He slid the rubber straps of the night vision goggles over his eyes, and he could see everything. He chuckled to himself. *Always come prepared,* he thought and sat in his little hiding place to wait.

She would be his very soon. He had caressed her with his eyes while she shopped. Kelly bought a piece of stalactite affixed to a base from the gift shop. The piece of rock glittered in the sunlight as she held it up. The tiny pieces of limestone that had smoothed to crystal clear gems imbedded in the stone helped it to catch the sunlight. She did not know what laid in wait for her in the cave. He was her God, and he was ready to ascend with her help.

* * * *

T. J. and Danny, her protectors, stood next to her, looking as if they were just tourists enjoying the day, but these men were on the job. Kelly could see their vigilance, their attention not only on her but also to the people around them, looking for anything out of the ordinary or for any sign of Jeff Callister. Soon, they heard the slow hum of the trolley coming back and went to stand in line to get on the ride into the cave. With hard hats on, they sat as they listened to the tour guide in the front of the trolley when he started to talk. They made their way slowly into the cave. Taggert sat next to Kelly and Danny right behind them.

"There aren't bats in here, are there?" Taggert whispered in her ear.

Kelly laughed and shook her head. "No, big, bad soldier man, there are no bats, and here I was thinking you weren't scared of anything."

"I'm not scared of bats," he denied. "They're just creepy, that's all."

"Big baby," was Danny's comment from behind.

T. J. threw him a glare, and Kelly laughed again. "Don't worry, Taggert, I'll protect you."

At the first turn, the sunlight was blocked out, and the dim lighting from the bulbs that lined the cave enfolded them. The wide entrance led into the most beautiful cavern. The sounds of water dripping and of the hot springs bubbling filled the air. Everyone in the tour gasped at the awesome sight in front of them. The walls of the cave glittered from the rock formations filled with limestone and crystals. The different colors of light that were used caused a wonderful rainbow contrast on the rocks. The tour went deeper into the caves, and as they went, Kelly pointed out certain aspects of the cave she remembered from taking the tours as a child. She turned around and talked to Danny after he threw questions her way. Soon they were in the section of the cave where the waterfall was. The water poured out of an opening near the roof of the cave into the crystal pool. The tour group was allowed to get out and walk around to see everything, including the plant life that grew in the cave. There the story was told about the man who found the cave in the early 1900s and for whom the cave was named after. Kelly had walked over to the water and leaned over the rail. Taggert was walking toward her while Danny stayed by the trolley when the tour guide announced to the tour members.

"And now, to show you how the cave looked when Harrison discovered it, we turn off the lights. Please stay by the pool. Some of this cave is not as yet fixed for viewing, and we don't want you to get lost. Ready? Hit them!"

"No, wait!" T. J. said but it was too late. The entire cave was pitch dark in an instant. A few women screamed, and some people giggled.

"Kelly!" T. J. called.

"I'm here," she returned the cry.

Kelly was standing by herself when the lights went off. She had forgotten this was part of the tour two minutes of complete dark. She felt alone in the dark then she felt the hand go around her neck, she tried to scream but a hand clamped over her mouth. She felt the terror rise in her. It was him! *It's Jeff Callister.* How'd he get in? He was not on the tour. Kelly opened her mouth and bit the hand that was across it then she screamed for her man.

"Taggert! Help me, it's J—" was all she got out before she went unconscious.

* * * *

"Kelly! Kelly!" T. J. called out frantically, pushing his way through people in the darkness trying to follow the place where he thought her voice came from.

"I can't see a fucking thing!" Danny yelled.

"Get those fucking lights on now!" T. J. yelled out the order as he moved when there was no move to get the lights on he yelled again.

"Police business, get those damn lights on!"

T. J. continued calling Kelly's name, but there was no response. The tour guide turned the lights back on as soon as he heard the yell about police. The cave filled with light, and people started looking around wondering what was happening. T. J. reached the place where he had last seen Kelly. Danny was by his side seconds later. There was no sign of her. The only thing they found was the piece of stalactite she had purchased in the box on the cave floor.

"Where is she, man? Where the fuck is she?" Danny heaved out.

Dread spread through T. J. as realization hit him "He has her, Danny. He's got Kelly."

* * * *

Kelly woke up to being carried through heavy underbrush. Little twigs slapped her face as he carried her like a heavy bundle of sugar cane over his shoulders. She began to struggle and tried to scream, but her mouth was taped closed. The hands carrying her like a sack of potatoes held her tighter.

"Stop struggling, Kelly, or I'll put you to sleep again," Jeff Callister warned.

She ceased struggling. She knew it was better to be awake and think, to be able to see where she was so she could escape.

"Good little dove, you know your place," he said approvingly. "Soon we'll be at a place I picked just for you."

Jeff Callister talked to Kelly as if he were talking over coffee with an old friend. His joviality amazed her. "You'll like the place I picked out. It has beautiful flowers. Big, wonderful blooms. They'll suit you, Kelly. I made sure it was perfect."

Kelly felt terror in its purest form at his words. In the swirling emotions, she tried to think about where he could be going and how she could leave a trail for Taggert to find. *Taggert, please find me,* she pleaded in her head, hoping the silent message could be communicated. But she knew if she were to be found, she would have to help herself.

Jeff's voice broke through her thoughts. "You know, I knew you were special. I wouldn't travel and hunt someone if she wasn't just right. For a minute, Kelly, you were hard to find, but just for a minute. Your lieutenant couldn't hide you for long."

His voice turned cold. "He touched you, he fucked you, didn't he? He soiled my perfect dove. For that, I must exact some sort of repayment from you. You didn't stop him. You let him make you his whore."

In the next moment, his voice turned cheerful again. "But, no matter, dear Kelly, the part of you I want he could not touch. Your heart is far away from that thing between your legs."

He is so wrong, Kelly thought, listening to the maniac ramble on and unable to say anything. Taggert had touched her heart more than anything else. Only now, she didn't know if she was ever going to get to see him again. *Please find me!* She thought again and closed her eyes to a branch that slapped against her face.

* * * *

T. J. was frantic, the police of the little island combed the caves with lights, and outside more armed officers searched the wooded areas surrounding it. Jeff Callister had planned his route well, and by the time the search started, he was long gone. Kelly's brothers had been called as soon as she went missing, and they were at the cave quickly. In less than half an hour, they walked up to T. J. and Danny. Tony could not control the anger that welled up inside him.

He gave T. J. a shove, sending him back against the wall of the visitor's center of the cave. T. J. was up in an instant, ready to fight the man. They were both worried and fearful about Kelly and her safety. If the only way to get some of that worked off so they could think was to come to blows, then so be it. T. J. was ready.

"You were supposed to protect her, to watch her. How could you let this happen, man?" Tony shouted trying to get back to T. J., but his brothers, both had worried looks on their face, held him back.

Danny restrained T. J. He shouted, "I was watching her. They turned off the damn lights. How was I to know they would . . ."

His voice broke on the last of the words, and he took a deep breath, nodding to Danny, who released him. In a calmer tone, T. J. continued, "I didn't know they would turn off the lights in the cave. If I had known, she would not have left my side, but she wanted to look in the pool. I thought it was safe."

He shoved his hand through his hair and looked at the brothers with agony written all over his face. "I'd do anything for her. I'd die for her and I'm going to kill the man that took her." He finished with deadly intent in his voice.

Tony had relaxed, and he, too, was released from his brothers' hold. Then Danny, seeing T. J.'s reaction, took the lead. "Guys, you know this area well, right?"

The three brothers nodded their heads in affirmation and Danny continued. "We don't think he took her too far. He'd have to have somewhere close planned out ahead of time in case he got her. It was just as a fucking coincidence that he got her here."

"Now all we need is a clue of the direction he took her in and we can search from there."

"I think we have that clue, Detective Greywood." The captain of the police walked over to Danny holding a large amber crystal and a few blue beads. "Are these the property of Ms. Justine?"

T. J. walked over and said excitedly, "Yes, my mom gave her that necklace. It must have broken when he took her!"

"One of men found them going off to Welchman Hall Gully."

"That is what?" T. J. asked impatiently.

"That, Lieutenant Chapel, is one of the largest gullies on the island with a few small caves in it. It could be nearly impossible to find him in there," the captain said.

"For people who don't know it," Max said, and everyone turned to look at the bothers.

"We used to play in there as children. We caught crawfish in there, caught rabbits, and picked fruits," Tim said.

"The one constant is that Kelly was with us all the time. We could never leave her out." Tony added.

"Told you we couldn't get rid of her," Tim said ruefully.

"So that means that she knows the area as well?" T. J. asked hopefully.

"Yes, we had a game where we all would take different routes to get out of the gully. Whoever made it back first won something of what belonged to the other person. She had a lot of our stuff."

"Good, good." T. J. felt hope fill him. "That means if she has the opportunity she'll run and all we have to do is find her when she does."

"Let's go to where they found the beads and we'll work from there," Danny said. The group of men started off toward the gully.

"Under his breath T. J. muttered, "Come on, sweet pea, run if you can. I'll find you, baby. I'm coming to find you."

* * * *

Jeff Callister moved quickly, but Kelly kept alert all through his ramblings about his ascension and immortality. She had managed to slide her bound hands under the necklace on her neck and break the cord that held it together. It hurt her neck, but it finally broke, and she let the beads dribble intermittently off her neck by holding her head down against the flow when she needed it to stop. She knew the beads would not last long, but she at least wanted to give a start of a trail for Taggert to find her.

God, Taggert, where are you? she thought. They were deep in the gully, and it was early evening. She knew this area well, had played here as a child, but not in the dark. She didn't think she could find her way in the dark. She hoped he'd stop soon so she could get a look around. As if hearing her wish, Jeff Callister stopped in a small clearing filled with wild hibiscus flowers and palm fronds. She looked around, and she saw that they were a few feet away from a bluff that went down to a small creek. Kelly remembered it from her childhood, from catching crawfish there with her brothers. Her brothers. She hoped they wouldn't give her parents details about her death and that they wouldn't grieve too long. *Shut up!* Her mind screamed. *You are not going to die!* Kelly knew she had some leverage. She knew this gully, but he didn't know that. She would play along as the frightened victim and, at the first opportunity, run. Even in the dark, she would keep running until she couldn't anymore.

He spoke to her gently as if she were his friend. "Kelly, I'm going to take the tape off now. If you scream, I'll slit your throat."

The calm way he said it made her skin crawl and she nodded that she understood his demand. He pulled the tape from her lips slowly enjoying the wince of pain she made as the sticky tape came off her skin.

"Thank you." She kept her voice small and meek, and Jeff inclined his head in acknowledgement. "May. . . May I have a drink, please?" Kelly said nodding in the direction of his canteen.

"Of course, my dove." He put the canister between her hands still bound by tape.

"Have a seat, Kelly, and we'll have a chat while I eat a little. It was a long wait, and breakfast was not for me this morning," Jeff said casually.

"I know you cook. I would have liked to taste your meals before I killed you." Her gaze flew to his face in terror, and he laughed softy. "No, no, not yet. We have a few things—well, I—have a few things to do before you die."

"Like what?" Kelly asked.

"Ah, ah, ah, that's my pleasure, not yours, little dove, but you can be sure that your lieutenant and the detective will die as well just not yet."

"Please, don't hurt them. You have me, I'm not fighting, I'm not running. They don't have to die," she pleaded.

"Oh, but they do. They made me fight for my prize. They're beneath me, and lesser men do not make me fight for what is rightfully mine."

Kelly got angry, and she lashed out at him in anger and in fear. "You're no god! You're a sick fucking man with a sick fucking mind! And you like hurting women. Even if you do kill me, I'll be laughing my ass off as a goddamn ghost because you'll still be human and a sick fucking freak! I'll have more power that you even in death!"

Jeff looked at her with interest in his eyes not even anger at her outburst, and then suddenly he clapped his hands delightedly. "Bravo, Kelly! I knew you had fire. That is why I picked you to be the final one. You are the fire to make me whole."

It was useless. He didn't even have a hold on reality anymore. "You're delusional, Captain Jeff Callister."

"So you know who I am, which means the lieutenant put the pieces together. How very clever of him. No matter, it's done. When I am immortal, I won't be a captain anymore. Here, drink some more Kelly. I don't want you passing out or anything. I need you good and hydrated when we start," Jeff said jovially. He was in a good mood.

Kelly on the other hand knew her time was running out. While Jeff Callister sat munching on crackers and cheese drinking from his canteen, Kelly sat with her hands hanging in her lap in between her legs and feeling around on the floor. She watched him as she felt around for what she needed a small flat stone that she could use to break the tape around her hands piece by piece. She had a plan as soon as her hands were free. She would find a way to get him down so she could run. Kelly found what she needed, a sharp flat rock, and she slowly began to rub it against the tape. Jeff looked at her, smiled, and went back to his meals. When he looked over, she palmed the stone, and then she began to work the tape once again. She would keep him talking and away from her until she could make a move.

Please find me when I run, Taggert. I'll be running to you, she thought as she worked on freeing herself.

Chapter Fifteen

"T. J., you've got to calm down man," Danny coaxed as they walked. He'd barely gotten the words out of his mouth when a palm frond hit him in the face after T. J. pushed past it. He grabbed T. J.'s arm and made him stop.

T. J. pushed past another palm frond. Daniel barely finished his sentence before the frond hit him in the face. Grabbing T. J.'s arm, Daniel made him stop and turn around.

"T-man, we have to move slowly so we don't miss anything. I know you're worried, but we'll find her."

"She's out there alone and scared. I have to get to her, Danny, because if anything happens to her . . ." T. J.'s voice took on a desperate edge one that Danny had never heard before.

"Easy, man, you have to pull it together. Remember, he's a soldier, and he's going to be using his training to evade you and keep Kelly. So you have to go into soldier mode too, even out the playing field."

T. J. took a deep breath willing himself to remember some of the missions he was on, remembering that without him Kelly would die. Tony ran up to them holding out his hand. "We found more beads. She's leaving us a trail! That's my Kellybear."

"Show me where," T. J. said, and they moved quickly to where the police were searching and Kelly's other two brothers waited.

"Looks like he's heading toward the creek," Tim said.

"How long is it?" T. J. asked.

"It runs the whole length of the gully."

T. J. took command then saying to the men gathered there, "Okay, everyone spread out, follow the length of the river. If anyone sees anything shoot one shot in the air. The rest of us will come running. Tony, Max, Tim, you guys search closer to this area. Danny, me and you will go down a little and work back this way."

"I am the captain here, Lieutenant Chapel," the police Captain started to say in an outraged voice. "You are an outsider. You cannot take authority over this situation."

"No, you're here because my government asked for your men to assist, that's it! That means this is my show, now if you have a problem with that, you take it up with my superior. Until then, if anyone stops me from doing what I'm doing, they will not be happy with my response." T. J. finished his little speech, coldly looking at each man. None could hold his gaze, and all recognized this was not a man to be trifled with.

* * * *

The thick metallic tape around Kelly's wrists was giving way. She could feel it every time another piece tore. She still moved slowly, not wanting to draw attention from her captor. He was talking to her about his plans when he left this mortal world, and she found out, to her horror, that his first kill was his mother. She had been the one who planted these ideas in his head as a child, and he thought it only fitting that her heart be the first to mark his beginning transformation. Through his conversation, Kelly worked to free herself. She looked around for a weapon, anything she could use to give a few seconds to run. She saw a large rock next to her, and she prayed that she could hit him without his catching wind of her plan. She looked at him as he finished off what was in his canteen and then started taking things out of a black duffle bag he had next to him. Kelly tried to talk with him, to reason with him for her freedom.

"Jeff, why are you doing this? Why me? Just let me go. I'll do whatever you want."

"So many questions, little dove, and an offer for whatever I want. Does that include the use of your body like the lieutenant has been given?" he asked her mildly.

The thought of his hands on her flesh brought bile to her throat and her skin crawled, but she answered as if it was her only choice. "If that's what it takes to get out of this," she said, knowing that she would die before giving him a chance to touch her like that.

He walked over to her and grabbed her hair pulling her head back cruelly causing Kelly to cry out in pain. "Are you such a slut to offer yourself up like some piece of meat? No matter, Kelly. It's not your body I want, just what's inside it that beats."

She looked at him defiantly even though his fingers were still wrapped tightly in her hair. "Should I listen to your heart and see what it says to me? Hmmm, Kelly? The human heart is the most amazing thing. It beats faster when it's scared and slow and rhythmic in sleep. What will yours say?"

"I hope it tells you how much I loathe you!" she spat out.

He let go her hair and kneeled beside her, placing his head on her chest to listen to her heat beat. Kelly closed her eyes as he laid his head against her. Jeff began to hum as if singing along to unheard music. She felt the last of the tape break—she was free! She slowed her breathing, willing her heart not to race. Kelly moved her hand slowly until she felt the rock under her palm. Curling her finger around the jagged stone, she brought it up quickly. Jeff Callister felt her move, but it was too late. He looked up just as Kelly brought the rock down against the side of his head.

Kelly didn't wait to see if she'd knocked him out. As soon as he slumped, she pushed as hard as she could and ran. She kept running, following the trail of the bluff. She screamed Taggert's name as she ran, hoping someone would hear her voice.

* * * *

"Did you hear that?" T. J. asked stopping Danny as they moved towards the creek.

"What? I didn't hear—" Danny said.

"There . . . There it is again! Kelly's screaming my name, come on!" T. J. shouted and began to run toward the scream.

"T. J. wait, there's a bluff before the creek!" T. J. was already gone through the bush shouting Kelly's name.

"Taggert!" She screamed again. "I'm here, Taggert, I'm here!"

"I hear her!" Danny yelled as he and T. J. were barreling through the dense foliage of the gully. T. J. was past caring what danger there was. He just had to get to her.

Kelly was running for her life now. She could hear Jeff Callister closing in on her. She dared not look back in case she tripped and fell. Each breath she took burned in her lungs from the exertion of her pace. She knew she couldn't slow down, and when she thought she was going to get away, she felt someone hit her back, knocking her to the hard dirt floor of the gully. Her breath whooshed out of her body, and then she was hauled over to lie on her back.

Jeff Callister straddled her body and he held a dangerous looking knife above his head. She could see the wicked glint of the metal in the waning light before he brought it down against the smooth tender skin of her throat. "You stupid bitch," he snarled at her.

Gone was the mildness with which he had spoken before. His face was contorted with cruelty, and his eyes glittered like cold emeralds, except now she could see the madness in them.

"I was going to spare you some of the pain! I was going to be benevolent. I was going to put you to sleep. Now I'm going to carve your heart out of you chest!"

Kelly screamed. This time it was the sheer terror that filled her throat. This was it. He was going to kill her and Taggert couldn't get there in time. She closed her eyes and silent tears slid out of the corners. She sent a silent I love you to Taggert and hoped she would go unconscious before he cut her open.

"Get off of her, you fucking bastard!"

The snarl came out of Taggert's mouth, sounding like a lion roaring in warning. To Kelly, it sounded like heaven. She turned her head to see Taggert standing at the opening of the clearing with his gun trained on Jeff Callister's head. Daniel came up next to him, and he, too, was armed and ready. She felt Jeff tremble a little at Taggert's cold stare. He pressed the knife harder against her throat until it pricked her and a drop of blood fell.

"Why, lieutenant, do you think you can shoot me before I slit this whore's throat?"

"I know this, I can sure kill you in the slowest ways possible. You're not the only one with training, Jeff Callister."

"That's Captain Jeff Callister to you, lieutenant," Jeff reminded him coldly.

"You're no captain. You're a dishonor to your corps and your rank. No man of honor does this to helpless victims. We are the ones who are supposed to protect. You're just a piece of slime that deserves to be in a hole for the rest of his life," T. J. said with disgust.

"You move that knife any farther, Jeff, and I'll shoot you everywhere other than where it will kill you," Daniel said softly but Kelly saw intent in his eyes clearly.

"You two will serve me," Jeff demanded. To Kelly, it was as if he was hoping that he could convince them this had to be done. The men could see that his madness had gone past all reality and he was in his own little world. Time seemed to slow down as she felt the steel blade against her throat. She focused her gaze on T. J.'s face. If there was one last thing she had to see before she died, it was the man she loved.

* * * *

Time to snap him back to reality, T. J. thought. "Uh, Jeff you can't transcend. You need your other hearts, and well, we have them."

Jeff's expression turned from surprise to extreme anger in seconds. "You don't have them," he snarled, his expression filled with malice.

"Oh yes, we do," T. J. continued, waiting for an opportunity to present itself so he could take Jeff down. "Yeah, we found your little attic room in your house, well the house you were renting, and we found those hearts in the jar. The guys laughed at the shrine you built to your mother's heart. They thought how pathetic is a killer who builds a shrine to his dead mother's heart. It's sad."

"I'm going to kill you," Jeff shouted. He sliced Kelly's arm, making her cry out in pain.

Jesus, T. J. thought, *I have to get his mind off her and on to me.* "You're going to kill me, huh?" T. J. snarled. "Well. How about you come on and try?"

"I bet the coroner is getting ready to cremate those hearts, then where's your immortality, Jeff? Or maybe we'll keep your mom's in a box somewhere, collecting dust until it rots away. Your mother must be so ashamed of you." T. J. made it sound like it was sadness in his voice.

"No! No, she's waiting for me, the mother of a god."

"Please, don't make me laugh," T. J. scoffed. "Wherever she is, she's probably denying you were ever her son."

"She probably wished she left you in a garbage can somewhere when you were born," Danny added in seeing where T. J. was going with this plan.

That was all it took. With a bellow of pure rage, Jeff Callister moved from straddling Kelly and rushed the two men. As soon as he moved, T. J. saw Kelly roll away and scramble to the side of a nearby tree. She was out of harm's way, and he could breathe.

As the man charged them, T. J. and Daniel did what they had to do and fired their weapons until he was on the ground bleeding. T. J. walked over and stood over the man whose breaths were shallow and uneven as the life drained from him. T. J. wondered if Jeff could hear his own heart beat slowing down, if it sounded like an echoing drum in his own ears.

T. J. spoke quietly, "You must be wondering how it came to be that you could be dying, huh?"

"But I was meant for immortality," he gasped.

T. J. looked down coldly at the man who had almost taken Kelly from him and felt no pity for him only sadness for the victims that lost heir lives because of him.

"No, you were meant to go to hell," T. J. said flatly and walked away.

Danny had already gone back the way they came to bring the rest of the search party to the scene. T. J. didn't even look back as he left Jeff Callister lying on the ground in a gully, dying not as a god, but as a man who was completely alone.

* * * *

As he walked toward Kelly, she ran to him, and he folded her in his arms, whispering words of reassurance to her that it was finally over. Agonizing over how close he had come to almost losing her, he kissed her face and her lips over and over again, making sure she was real.

"Oh, sweet pea, I'm sorry, so sorry," he moaned against her hair.

"No, don't be sorry. You found me, Taggert."

"It was my fault. I should have stuck close to you in the cave."

"No, baby. I forgot that they turned the lights off. If I had remembered, I wouldn't have walked away to the pool."

"God, Kelly, I thought I lost you. I love you so much. I don't know if I could've survived if anything had happened to you. I would have torn apart paradise to find you."

As Kelly framed his face with her hands, he closed his eyes against the tears that threatened to spill. She reassured him with her touch, a touch he almost lost. When he opened his eyes, she met his gaze, and he could see the love shining back at him.

"Taggert, you're never going to lose me. I'm here with you forever. I love you, too. More than words could ever say."

"From the first time you kissed me, Kelly, I found my paradise in you," he whispered.

The lovers sealed their love and their bond with a kiss while the island police swarmed around taking pictures. T. J. knew there was no place he would rather be than in Kelly's arms.

Against his lips, Kelly whispered, "Paradise found."

"Damn right!" T. J. responded and twirled her around in his arms.

Epilogue

Flowers and lace in the colors of wine red and cream decorated the backyard, and people milled around tables and danced to melodies that changed from slow and sexy to reggae every few minutes. On the dance floor, Danny danced with Abby, the maid of honor, dressed in a wine red dress. She looked petite in his arms, and from Danny's expression, he was having the time of his life. Looking handsome in tuxes with their braids running down their backs, Kelly's three brothers had the girls giggling with their flirtatious behavior. Kelly's parents were sitting at a table with her new nephew, born only a few weeks before.

T. J.'s mother watched her son and his new wife dance and whisper in each other's ears and pressed her hands against her chest. Maria looked away quickly, dabbing her eyes with a lace handkerchief, and Kelly's mother walked over to the woman putting her arms around her in a big hug. Tank the dog ran barking as children from Kelly's side of the family played with him and fed him things he was not supposed to have.

Then there was the couple, whom everyone was watching. Kelly and T. J. were wrapped in each other's arms and dancing a slow dance even though the music had changed to calypso. Six weeks before the clouds over their lives were dark and gloomy when T. J. thought he would lose the woman who held his love. They had gotten her away from the man who had stalked her for weeks. Jeff Callister's body had been buried without honors. Kelly and T. J. had come back to his lakefront home to plan a wedding and forget the nightmare that had plagued them. Now, on a beautiful December day, which was suprisingly warm even for a Carolina winter, they had exchanged their vows and were celebrating together with their families.

"Hey, what do you think of the reception?" Kelly asked, looking up into the eyes of her new husband.

"It's wonderful. I'm surprised you put it together so quickly," T. J. replied.

"Well with my family handling the cooking and your mom's help with the decorating and Abby's help with the—"

"Okay, okay, I get it. You had a lot of help." T. J. laughed.

"I'm just saying it was beautifully done," Kelly said in her Ms. Priss voice.

As they continued to dance, T. J. asked, "How do you like being Mrs. Kelly Chapel?"

"I like it very, very much, but do I get lieutenant in my title as well?"

"For that you have to work up the ranks," T. J. said wickedly.

"Why, Taggert, I thought I worked up your ranks well enough a few nights ago," Kelly responded sexily.

T. J. felt the heat go straight through him. She had the ability to make him want to throw her down and ravish her in the strangest places.

"Behave or you won't get your wedding present," he warned silkily.

"What wedding present? Where is it?" she asked excitedly.

"Oh, it should be arriving right about now."

There was a rumble of an engine, and the crowd looked over and went toward the lake to see what the commotion was. Then Kelly spotted a white craft down the lake.

"A boat! You bought me a boat!" She squealed, hiked up her wedding dress, and pulled him to the lake's edge.

"Yup, she's ours for when the weather gets warmer. We can cruise the small islands around the lake," T. J. explained with a laugh. "Or a least when we aren't in the Caribbean."

"I love it! I love it!" She clapped her hands and then smacked a huge kiss on his lips.

"Wait, Kelly, look at the name."

Kelly looked down at the letters on the boat written in the wine red and in script. He saw her eyes mist with tears. "Oh, Taggert, I love it, I love you."

"I love you too, sweet pea."

The name of the boat was *Paradise Found*.

About the Author

Dahlia Rose, best selling author of contemporary erotica, suspense and paranormal romance. She was born and raised on a Caribbean island and now currently lives in Charlotte, NC with her four kids who she affectionately nicknamed "The children of the corn and her biggest supporter/long time love. She has a love of erotica, dark fantasy, Sci-fi and the things that go bump in the night. Books and writing are her biggest passion and she hopes to open your imagination to the unknown between the pages of her books.

Amira Press, LLC

www.amirapress.com
books@amirapress.com

Behind Blue Eyes
by Pat Cromwell

Michael's goal is to have it all. Falling for the boss's daughter wasn't part of the plan. But some things are worth the risk, and she was it! Soon Michael is pitted against a man he once considered his mentor and Seine becomes an unwitting pawn in the game of cat and mouse between the two men. She quickly realizes she's in the position to end it. She just has to decide which team to play on. Will it be family loyalty or the man who owns her body and soul? Will she trust the love Behind Blue Eyes?

Amira Press, LLC
www.amirapress.com
books@amirapress.com

Mining Evermore
by Kathleen Rowland

Breezy black criminal attorney Tara Delacruz gets unpopular clients exonerated while her rival, the white-bread mayor and secret immortal, Cord Smith, wants them off his streets. Somewhere along their craggy coast, a fiend buries his victims at low tide at neck level. When the tide rises, they don't drown. Their town is spooked. Cord knows someone has found an evil use of immortality and believes the lawyer may have run across him. When he's forced to speak with her, he falls for the woman he censures. Bound to a secret conspiracy, he can't share everything, yet he warns her not to accept this twisted case.

Printed in the United States
106483LV00009B/169/P